Giblet & Belle

THE CASE OF THE
ONE STILL TOO MANY

Robert Lay

Text: Robert Lay
Editors: Emily Yau and Ashley Strosnider
Cover Design: Natalia Junqueira
Illustrations: Natalia Junqueira
Interior Design and Layout: Danielle Smith-Boldt

ISBN: 979-8-218-05297-3

Table of Contents

Epigraph

"He who is not contented with what he has,
would not be contented with what he would like to have."
—*Socrates*

"Until one has loved an animal,
a part of one's soul remains unawakened."
—*Anatole France*

Cast of Characters

Protectors–An ancient society of cats, working behind the scenes, always in the shadows, protecting mankind

Belle–A young black cat and Protector in training; Giblet's best friend

Mittens–A Mane Coon cat and senior Protector from an ancient line; leader of the clowder

Giblet–A fussy Tabby tomcat that wants worries about Belle, his best friend

Anne Gaumont–Retired senior police detective and neighbor to Giblet & Belle

Joel Grey–A Russian Blue cat, a member of the clowder who has a dark secret

Gus–Neighborhood tomcat and casanova; a perpetual flirt

Luther–Retired New York City police dog

Shirley Macgregor–Mom, (Woman-Person to the cats) and English Professor

Russell Macgregor–Dad (Man-Person to the cats) and History Professor

Cassidy MacGregor–Macgregor's daughter; who is in the fifth grade

Christopher Macgregor–Macgregor's son who is in the third grade

MacKayla–Shirley & Russell's first cat, a beautiful calico cat who is deceased

Iko–Australian Cattle dog and the family pet for the MacGregors'

Marie MacLearnan–Busby, WV. Librarian and Obidiah's niece

Obadiah MacLearnan–Mountain man, distiller, and lover of all animals

Porter–Highland Collie, born in Inverness, Scotland

Dolion Dubghall–Mayor of Busby, WV.

Lucinda–Dolion's white Persian cat

Jarred Hebeto–Busby's police chief and fixer for Dolion

Nathan Rose–Saloon owner and restaurateur, cousin to Marie MacLearnan

Prologue

Agnes always looked forward to the second Wednesday of the month. Instead of a frozen meal or a can of soup for dinner tonight, she might have a nicely prepared pork chop or a chicken breast. No matter how well she planned her budget, money was always tight the week before her Social Security payment hit her bank account. *But tonight will be different,* she thought to herself. *No potted meat tonight; I will eat like a Queen this evening.* She chuckled.

Agnes wasn't upset with her situation. She was eighty-nine years old and still getting around, albeit slowly. Her apartment was nice, there were good neighbors, and her church group looked after her. The Social Security and small retirement pension she received from the railroad meant she was comfortable. On the other hand, her parents were born during the Great Depression and told her about bread lines, soup lines, and shoes with Hoover leather, which was just cardboard to plug the holes. *I'm doing really well compared to what Mom and Dad had to put up with,* Agnes thought.

She wasted no time that morning walking to her neighborhood bank as soon as it opened. Agnes lived in Torrington, an old mill town in the heart of Connecticut. She withdrew about half of her Social Security deposit in cash; half of it would be for grocery shopping, and the rest would go in the sock drawer of her dresser for use later.

Her bank was constantly on her to get a debit card, but her response was always no thank you. First, cash was real, and it was something she could hold in her hand. Second, who could remember all those PIN numbers, usernames, and passwords that kept changing all the time? Two times she tried a debit card, and she was locked out of her account on both occasions. *No, thank you.* Finally, she just plain enjoyed going to the bank and talking to the tellers, who all knew her.

She was walking back to her apartment with fresh groceries in her basket and the rest of her money in her purse when a car with two young women pulled up to the curb. The teenage girl in the passenger seat rolled down the window and called her over, asking for directions. Of course, being older and living on your own makes you cautious of strangers. However, because they were girls, Agnes did not feel particularly threatened and moved toward the car to help; that's when a third teenager came rushing out from between the houses and made a grab at the strap of her purse.

Agnes was no shrinking violet. You didn't grow up with two older brothers, get married, and work around railroad men for sixty years without toughening up a little. In a testament to her stubborn Irish heritage and facing a much younger foe, she did the only thing she could think of. Agnes fell to the ground, curled herself around her purse, and let out a blood-curdling scream.

One street over, a young black cat sitting on a porch rail suddenly jumped to her paws...

CHAPTER I

The Offer

*"I have never known a cat to have trouble on speed-dial
like this one does," Mittens confided.*

8 Cat Hours Before...

"It was a gang initiation," the lead officer told Mrs. Gaumont as he made notes for his report. "Each one of them had to rob someone and bring whatever they stole back as proof.

How did you respond to this so quickly?" he asked.

"I was having my coffee on my porch when I heard the screaming," the former detective replied. "I grabbed my old service revolver and came over as fast as I could. When I got here, Blonde there," motioning to the handcuffed girl on the ground, "was trying to pry the handbag loose, and the other two in the car were yelling to hurry up. The real rough stuff hadn't started yet."

"What did you do when you arrived?"

"As soon as I got close, I pulled my revolver and ordered her to stop. The two in the car immediately took off and left Blonde. She tried to run, but she tripped. I held her here until you arrived. I have the car's license and make," Mrs. Gaumont said, handing a scrap of paper to the officer. "But I feel the one you have will not be interested in taking the fall by herself."

"You still have good ears to hear the screaming from a street over, Detective," the Officer observed with a smile. "Do you want your old job back?"

"Yes, my ears are still pretty good," she admitted, looking past the officer and smiling at two cats, one Maine Coon and one all black, sitting on the lawn next door watching the proceedings. "But these days, I like the quiet life. So, I think I will stay retired."

The officer was too busy taking notes for his report to pay attention to the two cats watching them. Even if he did try to pay attention to the cats, all he would have heard would be soft meows, and what to humans sound like purrs. However, he would have found the conversation illuminating if he could speak cat.

"How'd you trip her?" Mittens, the senior Protector, asked her apprentice.

"I ran under her feet and swiped at her ankles," Belle, the small black cat meowed. "It's instinct to try to step around an obstruction, not kick it," she purred. "Blonde lost her balance and fell over just as Anne arrived and ordered her to freeze. It wasn't long before the police appeared."

The police officer helped the handcuffed young woman to her feet. As he escorted her to the patrol car's back seat, he noticed a small group of onlookers had assembled across the street and were filming the proceedings with their phones; *typical,* he thought. Then he saw two cats sitting quietly in the neighboring yard watching the same events; *not typical,* he thought.

"Have you ever seen her around here before?" Belle asked, motioning with her paw to the suspect in the police car.

"No, she's not from around here that I know," Mittens purred. "The Police said it was a People gang initiation, so they probably came from an adjacent community."

Speaking from years of experience, the senior Protector suggested, "It's not a good idea to commit a robbery in your own neighborhood where People might recognize you."

"You did very well to hear this from our house," Mittens observed, complimenting her apprentice. "I missed it while I was in the house. However, when I heard the police sirens, I figured you would have a paw in these shenanigans."

"I was lucky that Anne was on her porch. She got right up and followed me when I told her there was trouble," Belle admitted, using Mrs. Gaumont's first name.

"Luck is one of the prerequisites of being a Protector," Mittens agreed. Then, looking at the suspect in the police cruiser, she added, "We will have to keep an eye out for this sort of thing in the future and shut it down quickly. I don't think we want our neighborhood to be used by gangs for these sorts of things in the future."

"You seem to have things well in paw here. So, I'll head home and let Giblet and Joel know everything is okay. You know how Giblet worries about you."

"See you at home," Belle agreed. "But I am going to listen for a little while longer."

Mittens stood and stretched, feeling a little stiff this morning. She was a ten-year-old Maine Coon; large, even for a large breed. She had long fur and a family history of being a Protector that went back centuries. Her family line could be traced to the court of King Louis XVI.

Looking at Anne and catching her eye, the Maine Coon meowed once and started for home. She was proud that Belle was alert and had thwarted the robbery. Her young apprentice was working out very well and becoming an excellent Protector, the ancient secret order of cats that had watched over and defended People and their settlements for thousands of years, mostly without humans realizing.

Mittens, the Queen of the clowder, was respected by all who knew her. They lived together with the same forever-family in the big white clapboard house in Torrington. In addition to being an extraordinary Protector in her own right, Mittens was also a teacher, mentor, friend, and beloved house cat to her People family.

Protectors could be found worldwide, wherever there were People and wherever there were cats.

Protectors started in Mesopotamia when the first organized People settlement were formed. From there, you could find them walking with the Pharaohs of ancient Egypt1 After that, they helped end the Black Death in the Dark Ages by eliminating the rats carrying the plague. Protectors also had a paw in stopping Genghis Khan at the kingdom of Hungary and turning him back at the gates of Vienna, the exact details of which are lost to history.

Protectors worked behind the scenes in countless People's wars to limit the damage and deaths. For example, a Protector was involved in the American Revolutionary war. The cat, Cressida, was the house pet of the only woman in General Washington's spy ring, code-named 355.

During the American Civil War, a Protector was with President Lincoln in the White House and thwarted several attempts on the President's life. Staff would remark that Lincoln would spend hours talking to the cat named Tabby and described how Tabby had the run of the White House, including the war cabinet. President Lincoln fed the cat at the dinner table with a gold fork, resulting in many a raised eyebrow from the other dinner guests.

Protector lore said that Tabby uncovered the plot to assassinate President Lincoln but was prevented from accompanying the President to Ford's Theater. It is worth noting that Tabby never forgave herself for not preventing the President's assassination and soon dropped out of sight.

---

1   Fun fact, cats were considered to be Gods by the ancient Egyptians. The cats didn't mind.

New Protectors are always female and are always called to duty by the current guardian of the district, region, or town. A potential recruit would be approached when the correct qualities were observed, and an offer would be tenured. Cat lore said that no cat ever turned down the offer of training to be a Protector except one.

Belle was the youngest cat in the clowder and Mittens's apprentice Protector in training. Small for her age but with strength and agility that rivaled cats twice her size, Belle had a thirst for knowledge and a desire to prove herself.

The other two cats in the house were Joel Grey and Giblet. Old Joel Grey was a handsome, sixteen-year-old Russian Blue who had come to the family a little over ten years ago. He was the most senior cat since MacKayla passed, about sixteen human years old, and spoke with a thick West Virginia accent.

The last cat that made up the clowder quartet was Giblet, a tabby tomcat with a pink nose, perfect fur, and dignified *(if he did say so himself)* coloring. Belle had teased Giblet more than once, calling him Mr. Fussy Paws because of his querulous nature, but in reality, he had a heart of gold. He was Belle's best friend and worried incessantly about her being a Protector.

Mittens arrived back home and went inside to find Giblet. He was in the family room when she located him.

"Belle is fine, the police are there, and Anne took care of the heavy lifting," she reported to the apprehensive tomcat.

"Belle is always sticking her nose into some kind of trouble around the neighborhood," Giblet bemoaned. "It really seems like there are more problems around here than there used to be."

"No, I don't believe there are more problems around the neighborhood than before. It's just that our young Protector seems to find what crime there is with ease," Mittens speculated. "I have never known a cat to have trouble on speed-dial like that one does."

"Well, I don't like it," Giblet grumbled as he lay down for his morning nap. He wouldn't fall asleep, however, until Belle was home safe.

That evening, the family returned home from their respective days; both Adult-People worked at the local college as professors, and both People-Kittens went to elementary school. Since the school dismissed before either parent was home, the kids stayed next door at Mrs. Gaumont's house until one of the parents could pick them up.

Anne and her husband never had children. However, being able to help watch Cassidy and Christopher Macgregor had drawn her into this family. Anne loved the children, and the whole family had begun to refer to Anne Gaumont as Grandma. She cheerfully accepted her new title and responsibilities.

Belle and Giblet hung around in the kitchen while the People made dinner, careful to avoid the dog Iko. It wasn't that Iko was in any way mean to the cats; it was just that if a piece of food dropped to the floor, you didn't want to be between the dog and the tasty morsel. While this was going on, Old Joel slept on the couch next to Mittens. She was trying not to draw attention to the fact that she was reading the evening newspaper sitting next to her. You see, cats can read, only they would rather the People around them not know.

Everyone took their places for dinner, the cats sitting on the family room couch and chairs while Iko paced anxiously near the People-Kittens, always in the hope of a handout. Despite their schedules, the Woman-Person and Man-Person thought it was essential to have at least one meal together as a family.

This evening, the Man-Person had an announcement concerning the whole family and their summer plans. First, he produced a letter that he'd got at work that day. Then, with a theatrical flourish, he began to read aloud.

Dr. Russell Macgregor, PhD.
Department of History
Torrington College, Torrington Connecticut

Dear Sir,

We are pleased to announce that the Grant Proposal for your book, The History Of Illicit Whiskey Production In The United States, 1900 To Present, has been approved. Congratulations.

In addition, the summer appointment for your wife, Dr. Shirley Macgregor, PhD., has been confirmed by the English Department, Busby College, Busby, West Virginia.

"Finally," the Woman-Person said. "You've been working on this for how long?"

"Over two years and counting," he admitted.

"What about us and the animals?" the little girl, Cassidy, asked.

"We are renting a house for the summer, so everyone is going, including the animals," the Father-Person responded. "Your mother and I talked it over and invited Grandma Gaumont to come along. So, she can watch you two while we are at work."

"Anne will enjoy the trip," The Woman-Person confirmed. "She hasn't had a vacation since Mr. Gaumont passed away several years ago. It will be good for her to get out of the house for a while."

Cassidy slid off her chair and rushed over to pick Giblet up in a big bear hug. "Isn't this great, Giblet! We're going on vacation," she sang as she danced around the room with the reluctant tomcat. Iko circled them both and barked, unsure what they were celebrating but happy to celebrate nonetheless.

Belle was trying to smother her laughter at seeing how uncomfortable Giblet was right now. Some of it was because Giblet would rather not be dancing around in Cassidy's arms, but most of it was because Iko would get wound up, and there was no telling what she would do. The rest of his unease was because he did not like to travel and loathed the cat carrier.

Mittens sat and thought about who would watch the neighborhood while she and Belle were away. Finally, she decided to talk to a few other cats that might lend a paw and keep an eye on things. She would also ask Mac, the retired New York City Police dog, to help out. Mac was a German Shepherd with a head the size of a horse. He lived a couple of streets over and still remembered all his police training. Mittens knew that the last thing a criminal wanted was to be confronted by Mac.

The People and most of the animals were so caught up in their thoughts and planning for the trip that none of them saw the look of abject terror on Old Joel's face, but Belle did. The old Russian Blue had a thousand-mile stare, and his right paw was shaking.

Seeing the look of fright on his face, Belle walked over and patted Joel on the shoulder. "What's wrong, Joel?".

"Nuthin…Nuthin young missy. I musta eaten something sour, an' my gizzard is actin' up. I'm goin' to lay down," the old cat responded. Then, shakily, Joel walked out of the kitchen and headed upstairs. Belle watched him go but knew that whatever was bothering Joel, it wasn't "nothing."

Weeks turned into days, and finally, the family was ready to leave for their trip. Planning to leave early the next day, the Woman-Person and Man-Person packed the van the night before. They had given a house key to a Teaching Assistant in the Woman-Person's English Department. The grad student would live in the house while they were gone. She would pick up the newspaper and mail and forward the essential things to West Virginia.

Mittens and Belle had made their last patrol of the neighborhood and had asked several cats to keep an eye on things. These cats weren't

Protectors, but working together, they would alert People if something was amiss. Mac had also agreed to keep a watchful eye on the neighborhood.

"I gotcha covered, Mitts," the big German Shepherd woofed. "Ain't no one gonna start trouble with me around."

On their way home, Gus, the local tomcat, popped out of the bushes on their way home to say farewell. He was a little rounder and had gone grayer, but he was still a scoundrel and quite the ladies-cat.

"Oh, Mittens, I don't know what I am going to do without you all those cat-weeks you are gone," Gus lamented with exaggerated bravado. "You know that young white cat has been giving me the eye. But, with you gone, I may not be strong enough to keep saying no."

Mittens flattened her ears as Belle burst out laughing. It was just the reaction Gus liked to get out of the Maine Coon.

"First of all, Gus," Mittens began, "You can't do without what you never had in the first place. Second, that white cat is less than half your age. Third, you could be her grandfather."

"Mittens, you wound me. But, you know you are my one and only true love," he said melodramatically.

"Gus, you love pasta more than any particular female," the Maine Coon purred.

Belle watched the interplay between the two old friends, thoroughly enjoying it. The banter reminded her of the old Hepburn and Tracy movies her People liked so much.

Gus turned to leave and meowed over his shoulder, "Be safe, my love, and Belle, make sure you bring her back to me."

Belle smiled and said she would keep Mittens safe.

"Bye, Gus, and lay off the white sauces for a while," Mittens purred. "See you in September."

After reaching their yard, Mittens and Belle sat on the back porch for a minute and listened to the night.

"I guess we are as ready as we can be for the trip," Mitten reflected. "I just have never been away from my neighborhood for such a long period."

"Don't worry," Belle chirped. "We have let the right animals know we will be gone, and they promised they would keep an eye on things. We will be back in a few cat months anyway and back on patrol."

But then, becoming thoughtful, Belle asked, "Have you noticed that Joel is not looking forward to the trip?"

"Joel is from somewhere around West Virginia. He left for some reason and probably isn't very excited about returning," Mittens postulated. "He has always been closemouthed about his time before coming to this home, so whatever it was must have affected him pretty hard for him to make such a long journey.

"Still, it's been over ten cat years, so I doubt anybody remembers him. I looked at a map, and West Virginia is a bigger State than Connecticut," Mittens added. "I think the odds of running into someone who knows Joel are remote.

"We will just support him and be there if he needs to talk," Mittens summed up. "Well, little one, it's late, and we have a big day tomorrow. And, if you don't go and let Giblet know you're safe, he won't get any sleep."

Belle nodded, and the two Protectors went inside to get some rest.

Belle looked at the People clock for what must have been the dozenth time and saw it was three in the morning. When she had returned from her patrol, Giblet lifted his head, smiled, then let out a long sigh. Now, he could finally get some sleep.

The young Protector was curled up next to her best friend and tried to relax, but she found sleep elusive. She was excited about the trip, and she couldn't settle her mind. She wondered how long it would take to get to West Virginia, what their summer home would be like, and what she and Mittens would do all summer without a neighborhood to patrol.

Before she could close her eyes again and try for some sleep, she noticed dust in the air. Dust certainly wasn't unusual in the old house, but what drew Belle's attention was that this dust wasn't hanging in the air like usual; it was gently swirling into a vortex above her head. Furthermore, it did not have the colorless hue of house dust; instead, it looked like multicolored glitter, similar to what the little Person used in her art projects. But, unlike glitter, it was giving off its own gentle glow.

Belle was about to wake Giblet to see what he thought of this when a face became defined in the cloud. Dust coalesced into eyes, ears, and whiskers. It was a cat's face.

Belle stared guardedly at the face, wondering if she was dreaming. Then, as the face became more defined, recognition followed; it was a face from an old video on the Woman-Person's smartphone. It was MacKayla.

The old tabby cat was the family's first rescue after they were married and the matriarch of the clowder. She had welcomed Joel Grey, Mittens, and Giblet's arrival into the family. She had a paw in everything the family did and was a comforting presence. Mittens had once commented that it was MacKayla she always turned to with a problem.

MacKayla had lived to be over eighteen human years old, well over a hundred in cat years. Unfortunately, MacKayla passed away just before Belle joined the family. Based on the stories she heard from the cats that knew her, Belle always regretted that she never got to meet her.

Belle didn't think to wake Giblet. When the image began to speak, it was not with words. The cat's mouth never moved. Instead, Belle heard it in her mind.

"Belle, listen to me. I haven't much time. Joel will be in danger. You and Mittens must protect and help him," the voice in her head declared.

"What do you mean?" Belle meowed out loud, not knowing if MacKayla could read her thoughts.

The vision of MacKayla did not acknowledge the question but instead continued, *"You must help keep him safe."* Belle looked closely at the spectral image and noticed the strain it was taking to keep this doorway open. Then, as if MacKayla had run out of energy to keep the portal open, she began to fade away, and the glitter disappeared into the night. The room was once again dark and still.

"What? Did you say something?" Giblet mumbled, not fully waking up.

"No," Belle whispered. "Go back to sleep."

Did I imagine this? Was I dreaming? the young black cat wondered. Nothing in her Protector training had prepared her for this, leaving Belle quite shaken. The only thing she was sure of was that she wouldn't be getting much sleep the rest of the night and that she needed to talk to Mittens about it in the morning.

CHAPTER II

The Journey

"STOP HIM, BELLE!" Mittens ordered…

Cat Coordinates 40.2732° N, 76.8867° W
The Man-Person's alarm went off an hour earlier than usual, catching most of the house's residents off guard. The Woman-Person, Children, cats, and the dog displayed various levels of grumbling but then got about the task of preparing to leave on the trip.

"We have a long drive today. We need to get going," the Man-Person called, rallying the troops. The exceptions were Giblet, who flatly refused to lift a paw until he had breakfast, Joel Grey, who seemed to be missing, and Belle, who was already up.

Belle had risen with the dawn and rushed downstairs, searching for one of the People books in the living room: *Studies in Parapsychology–A ClinicalVviewpoint*. She was trying to find out if there was any basis for her experience last night. Unfortunately, the book was far too big to be able to read quickly. However, after skimming a couple of chapters, she concluded the term "apparitional experience" closely fit what she had undergone. *I will talk to Mittens when I can get her alone; she will know what to do,* she thought to herself.

The Woman-Person started the kids on their cereal in the kitchen and put kibble down for all the cats and dry food for Iko. The Man-Person was standing at the counter, pouring himself a cup of coffee, when there was a knock on the backdoor. "That will be Anne. She's never late."

He let Mrs. Gaumont in and then went outside to begin loading suitcases into the van.

Belle glanced at Joel's untouched food and meowed a question to Mittens and Giblet.

"Where's Joel?"

"He's hiding," Giblet responded between mouthfuls. "He still doesn't want to go."

"I will look for him when we're done," Mittens announced.

"I'll go with you," Belle purred, thinking this would be a good opportunity to tell her about last night.

As soon as everyone —human, cat, and dog— finished their meals, Mittens began hunting for Joel. The search was short; she found him almost immediately under the bed in the Old-Person's bedroom.

Seeing Mittens and Belle, Joel proclaimed with a loud meow, "I ain't a-goin'." He backed deeper under the bed. When Mittens began questioning him about his behavior, he gave off a soft hiss that made her stop and raise an eyebrow.

"Seriously, Joel?" was Mittens' only response.

It was the first time Belle had ever heard the old grey cat show disrespect to anyone, let alone Mittens. Before she could follow up with a question of her own, the Children and Mom-Person came into the room with one of the two large cat carriers.

Cassidy reached under the bed, grabbing the reluctant Russian Blue and bringing him to the carrier the Mom-Person had placed on the floor. Angry as he was and meowing loudly, Joel did not try to bite or scratch the little Girl. Consequently, he was unceremoniously pushed into the carrier, and the door was quickly shut. The Mom-Person picked up the carrier, and she and the kids went downstairs.

"Well, that wasn't like Joel," Mittens observed after a moment, mostly speaking to herself but seeing Belle nod in agreement.

Alone in the room at last with Mittens, Belle saw her opportunity to confide in Mittens about what she'd seen last night.

"Uh, Mittens, something extraordinary happened last night. I think it is somehow related to why Joel is so upset," Belle began tentatively.

Mittens turned, giving her full attention to Belle. The student began haltingly, talking about her inability to sleep and the excitement about going on the trip. But then, the whole episode gushed forth, seeing the ephemeral vision of MacKayla and repeating what the apparition said. Mittens listened, frowning a little but not interrupting, the perfect listener.

"—I asked MacKayla what she meant, but all she said was Joel was in danger, and we had to protect him," Belle said. "The funny thing was, I think I heard MacKayla in my head, not through my ears. Then, this morning, I found a phrase explaining this in one of the People's books; it's called an "apparitional experience," but the book said it probably wasn't real."

Mittens stayed quiet when Belle finished. Then, uncomfortable with her mentor's silence, she asked, "What do you think it means? Did I imagine it?"

The Protector thought for a moment. Although Belle had seen Mittens angry, patient, and even amused a few times, this was the first time she ever saw Mittens unsettled; it bothered her.

"First of all, I don't believe you imagined it," Mittens said with conviction. "You remember the lesson about cats being able to catch glimpses into the next world?" Mittens paused, glancing up to see Belle nod, then continuing. "I am sure that is what you saw, the next dimension after this one. Of course, people cannot see this next universe, which is why the People book doesn't take it seriously.

But, usually, it is just a glimpse, never like the kind of visualization you experienced or duration you are speaking of. This is the first time I have heard of a cat being strong enough to make contact with this world. MacKayla's Chi must have been powerful," Mittens mused.

"Why did MacKayla contact me and not you?" Belle asked. "After all, you knew her, and I didn't."

"I don't know," came Mittens's reply.

"Could Anne see this plane? After all, she can understand Cat." Belle asked.

"I don't know...Good question, though," came Mittens' reply.

The Protector grew quiet again, deep in thought. Then coming to a decision, she meowed, "I want you to ride in Joel's carrier on the trip. I will ride with Giblet."

"You know he won't like that," Belle purred. "You intimidate him."

"Giblet will get over it. I want you to see if you can gently get Joel to open up about why he is so worried about returning to West Virginia. MacKayla picked you for a reason, and we need to understand why. You are less intimidating than I am. He might confide in you. We need more information if we are to be effective Protectors," Mittens finished as they both headed downstairs.

The journey began with Iko barking in her crate, Giblet meowing in his carrier while Mittens glared at him, and both kids sitting next to Mrs. Gaumont, trying to talk simultaneously. The din rattled Joel's nerves; Belle felt him shaking in their shared carrier. She casually tried to reassure him it would be okay and perhaps start a conversation. But Joel ignored her and continued staring out the carrier door. Gradually, everyone settled down as the Man-Person drove the van south, listening to his favorite classical music.

The van made good progress down Connecticut, across New York, then into Pennsylvania on Highway-81. Looking at the time, the Woman-Person suggested they should think about lunch and a bathroom break. The Man-Person said Harrisburg looked like a nice place and took the exit. Knowing they could not leave the animals alone in the van, they searched for a fast-food restaurant where they could get carryout and perhaps walk Iko a bit.

After they parked, the Woman-Person took everyone's order. One by one, they each called out what they wanted, including Giblet, who meowed loudly, *french fries!* The Woman-Person smiled at the tabby-cat and said, "I will get you something, Giblet, don't worry." While she picked up the food, the Man-Person walked Iko, and Mrs. Gaumont took the kids to the restroom.

Belle had tried to engage Joel in conversation throughout the trip, but the old grey cat ignored her, seeming to be asleep. Finally, Mittens looked at Belle with a raised eyebrow as if to ask, *did you learn anything?* Belle shook her head and settled back down.

When the Woman-Person returned, she handed the food out to everyone while the Man-Person put a bowl of water down for Iko. Next, she got some kibble and a couple of small milk cartons. She put a small portion of kibble in each carrier and a small bowl of milk as a treat.

She opened Mittens and Giblet's carrier and placed the bowl of milk inside. Giblet looked at the Woman-Person, then sadly down at the food, and finally, back up at the woman. *This isn't french-fries!* he meowed sadly.

Next, the Woman-Person opened Joel's and Belle's carrier to give them their food, when without warning, Joel's eyes popped open, and he launched himself out of the crate and leaped through the van's open door.

Belle was taken entirely by surprise. She had assumed Joel was asleep. Mittens banged against the door of her carrier, letting out an incredibly loud meow, startling everyone. What the animals heard was: "Belle, stop him!"

Belle sprang out of the carrier and chased Joel across the busy parking lot. Joel was cunning, cutting left and right, but nobody in the clowder could match Belle for outright speed and grace. She quickly caught up to Joel and leaped into the air, landing squarely on his back, tripping him up.

Both cats somersaulted on the pavement, ending up just the way Belle wanted, with Joel under her and with her teeth clamped securely down on the scruff of his neck. The way she had him, he could not get up to keep running.

"Git-offa me, ya dang cat!" Joel caterwauled, in between hiss and spits.

"Not a chance," she purred back, holding him tight.

Shortly the Man-Person and Woman-Person caught up, grabbing both cats.

"It looks like we have a runner," the Man-Person chuckled as he carried Joel back to the van.

"He's not used to car trips," the Woman-Person suggested. "Let's crate him with Mittens. She will control him."

Back at the van, they moved Giblet in with Belle and stuffed Joel in with Mittens.

"Are you okay?" Giblet asked with concern.

"I'm fine. I just wish I knew what was wrong with Joel," she purred back.

Joel lay down but would not look Mittens in the eye.

"When we get to West Virginia, you are going to tell me why you are acting this way," Mittens softly hissed. "And, I will not settle for the sleepy, good ole boy act."

Joel gave no indication he heard her. He just lay down and closed his eyes. When the van pulled back onto the highway, he began to shake again, ever so slightly.

CHAPTER III

Busby, West Virginia

"And, I wus the one who killed him,"
the old grey cat sobbed.

8:37, Eastern Standard Cat Time

A van full of exhausted Children, adults, and pets arrived at their destination, the quaint town of Busby, West Virginia, just as the sun set below the surrounding hills. All in the van were glad that the journey was over. The Man-Person said a silent prayer in his head, thankful that the return trip was three months away.

The town was nestled in a green valley on the Allegheny Plateau in the center of the county, and the Allegheny Mountains dominated the eastern horizon. The town was laid out along one long main street, going up the valley's center. Busby College anchored one end while a number of businesses lined the middle. The police department, city hall, and town square anchored the other end of town, with smaller streets branching off Main Street. These side streets held many of the town's original homes. A small stream meandered through Busby, passing under Mainstreet and disappearing around a bend in one of the surrounding hills.

The van doors opened into the hot, humid air of late spring. The Man-Person got out of the driver's seat and stretched, his back and shoulders popping. Likewise, the Woman-Person got out and stretched, happy the drive was at an end.

Before the Woman-Person could reach the handle, the sliding door on the van opened, and the Children piled out, wide awake and ready to work off some energy. The last to exit the van was Grandma Gaumont; following the lead of the others, she stretched to work the kinks out. Then, lifting her arms above her head, her blouse crept up, revealing a small black concealed-carry holster on her hip. The Woman-Person noticed the gun and raised her eyebrow.

Anne saw the Mom's eyes looking at her and knew what had attracted her attention. So, she casually replied: "For me, it's like grabbing a cell phone on your way out the door. Before I retired, I never went anywhere without my service weapon. But don't worry, I have a gunlock for it when I go to bed or leave it in the house.

The Woman-Person shook her head and said with complete honesty: "I'm not worried. You were a trained professional, and there isn't anybody I trust more to carry a gun than you."

Anne smiled at the compliment, picked up Iko's leash, and led her out of the van.

The Children wanted to run and explore the house that was their temporary new home, but the Father-Person said they had to take care of the pets first. Then, as if to echo that point, Giblet let out a long, loud plaintive meow from his carrier. Everyone laughed at the tabby cat's displeasure.

Inside the carrier, Giblet's howl was even louder. Belle looked at her friend and said with a grin, "I think they heard you back in Connecticut, Giblet."

"Dinner was supposed to be three hours ago. This is cat abuse!" he wailed.

"Your stoicism is impressive, Giblet," Mittens observed from the neighboring carrier, and Belle giggled.

Before they could start getting the cats out, an old Ford F100 pulled into the yard, with a woman behind the wheel and a full-size Highland

Collie in the passenger seat next to her. The woman parked the truck and leaned out the window: "You must be the Macgregor family. Welcome! I'm Marie MacLearnan."

"Yes, we are. I'm Russell, and over there is my wife Shirley," Shirley waved her hand in a friendly greeting as Russell walked toward the truck. "It's nice to finally talk to you in person and not just over the phone—."

"Thank you for arranging the rental of the house for us." Then, glancing back at the white clapboard house, he continued, "The house looks like it will work out great."

"No problem," Marie replied with a smile. "This house used to belong to my uncle, but he rarely stayed here; he preferred his cabin up on the mountain—.

Since I have my own place, this house sits empty unless I find a responsible boarder. I'm glad someone will live here this summer," Marie said as she got out of her truck, leaving the door open for the dog to follow.

Switching gears, Marie pointed, "The town library and historical center are right down the road, next to city hall. Almost everything in town is within walking distance, including the grocery store and the pharmacy. In fact, the mayor lives in the house two doors down, and I live several houses further up the road. Many of us walk to work each day."

She fished the key out of her pocket, handed it to Russell, then walked over to see Iko, who was tugging at the leash and wagging her tail so fast she created a breeze.

"Hi, I'm Anne," Mrs. Gaumont said, extending her free hand. "I'm a family friend and will take care of the kids while the professors are at work."

"Pleased to meet you, Anne," Marie replied.

While they were talking, the old Highland Collie came over and sat next to Marie. "And, this is Porter. He wants to say hello," she said with a smile.

"Hi Porter," Anne said, bending down to let the Collie sniff her hand when another meowing complaint erupted from Giblet in the van.

Marie turned her head to the van as Anne said, "The peanut gallery is hungry."

"Hush, Giblet," Belle purred. "I want to hear this Person."

Giblet harrumphed once more, then lay down while Belle and Mittens listened to the conversations, wishing they could see the new dog and its owner. Then, without warning, Marie poked her head in the van's door and looked at all the cats.

"Hi there," Marie said with a smile, then paused to look at Joel Grey, a flicker of recognition in her eyes. For his part, Joel stared back and then moved behind Mittens in the carrier.

Iko and the Highland Collie continued to exchange sniffs. Then, Iko bounced back and forth, wanting to engage the Collie in play, but the older dog looked distracted and simply sat and sniffed the air, taking in deep breaths of the various scents.

In an excellent mimic of a Person thinking deeply, the Highland Collie cocked his head to the side, satisfied. Porter woofed once, then sat quietly, looking at the van.

"Ghost?" Belle exclaimed, having heard what the dog had said. "Why, ghost?" she purred softly to Giblet and Mittens.

Giblet shrugged, and Mittens shook her head, admitting she didn't understand the reference either. However, she was fascinated by Joel's reaction; he began shaking at the word 'Ghost.'

Marie looked into the van one more time, but she couldn't see him very well anymore because of the encroaching darkness. Finally, she said, walking away from the van, "You know what. That Russian Blue looks like a cat my uncle had many years ago. He and that cat were inseparable."

"What was the cat's name?" Anne asked, making conversation.

"Oh, his name was the Grey Ghost, or just Ghost, for short. He disappeared around the same time my Uncle went missing," Marie said with a touch of sadness.

Inside the van, the mention of the name Ghost had a different effect on each cat. Giblet looked confused, Belle and Mittens contemplative, and Joel looked terrified.

"Isn't 'Ghost' the name that strange dog just said?" Giblet whispered to Belle.

"Yeah," Belle confirmed.

Anne said sympathetically, "I'm sorry to hear about your uncle. This cat's name is Joel Grey or just Joel."

"Pleased to meet you, Joel," Marie called into the dark van before walking to her truck with Porter. "We're going to get going. I'm sure you have a lot of unpacking to do. When you get settled, Russell, come to the library. I can set you up in a spare office so you can start your research."

"Thanks for everything," the Man-Person called.

The old truck backed out and disappeared up the street as the Woman-Person and Man-Person opened the front door of their temporary home and began carrying in bags.

More by luck than design, the house had a fenced backyard for Iko. Anne took her there and let her loose. She immediately began running around and sniffing her new enclosure.

The Man-Person carried the cat crates into the house and up to the Master Bedroom while the Woman-Person set up a litter pan and put out water and kibble. She opened both carriers and then closed the bedroom door as she left.

Giblet immediately walked over and began eating while Belle drank some water. Mittens emerged from her carrier and reached out with both front paws, stretching while extending her claws and yawning. She sat down and began putting her fur back in order when she noticed Joel had not come out. Looking in, she saw the old grey cat curled up in a ball at the back of the carrier.

"You will have to come out of the carrier eventually, Joel," Mittens offered gently. "I think it's time you told us what is going on."

Belle padded over to sit next to Mittens, staring into the carrier.

"We are your forever-family, Joel," Belle meowed. "Whatever it is, we will help."

"You can't help this youngin," came the soft, sad reply from the carrier.

"Tell us. We only want to know," the little black cat pleaded.

"I never wus gonna set paw in this place ever again," Joel lamented.

"You might as well talk, Joel. You know these two won't give you a moment's peace until you do," Giblet purred.

Reluctantly, Joel turned around and came to the door of the carrier.

All three cats got comfortable and looked at Joel expectantly. Finally, the old cat took in a deep breath and let it out as a sigh.

"Ya see, my first Person wus killed. That's why I had ta leave Busby." The grey cat sobbed. "And, I wus the one done killed him."

Belle, aghast, shook her head in disbelief and denial. Giblet, to his credit, held his tongue, waiting for more information. Only Mittens got a scowl on her face, saying in effect, *I don't believe you.*

Seeing their reaction, Joel said, "It's true. My person, Obadiah, would still be alive if it weren't fer me."

"Why don't you start from the beginning," Mittens purred.

Joel took a deep breath and gazed into space as the rest of the cats got resettled.

CHAPTER IV

Obadiah & the Grey Ghost

"You all are makin' a mistake. I hope you reconsider."

Ten People Years before, Mid-Fall— Lunar Cat Calendar.

The man leaned back in the old wooden rocking chair on his porch and put his feet on the rail. There was no telling how old the chair was, or the man for that matter. Both bore the indications of sustained use without much in the way of upkeep.

Obadiah wasn't young. Once chestnut brown, his hair and beard were now streaked with liberal amounts of grey. His exposed skin had the appearance of tanned leather, and his powerful hands bore many callouses. Only the eyes did not seem to go with the rest of his countenance. Bright blue, with a hint of whimsy, they looked like they belonged to a much younger man. Those blue eyes especially twinkled whenever he saw his niece Marie, he was taking care of his animals, or making his whiskey.

Marie was his sister's kid, and although he did not raise her, to Oba, she was the daughter he never had. She and her mother made frequent trips to the cabin while growing up. Oba taught his niece about the mountain, the animals who lived there, and whiskey making. When Marie started college, her trips to the cabin became less frequent. However, when she was home from college, she always hiked to the cabin for a visit.

On those visits, Marie would scold Obadiah, telling him to take better care of himself. She would bring him treats for his animals and generally fussed over him. After his sister passed away a few years before, Marie became his only living relative.

Outward appearances meant very little to Obadiah. Clothes, food, and housing were functional and certainly not benchmarks to judge oneself. Besides Marie, the two things that mattered to Oba were his animals and making his whiskey.

The care he provided for any creature in need wasn't a burden but rather was nourishment for his soul. And often, those animals would return the love ten fold.

The only thing Oba wanted, needed to be perfect, was his whiskey. He and his ancestors had been making the finest sipping whiskey that anyone had tasted in the hills of West Virginia for over the last hundred years. That is why a bottle of MacLearnan Special Reserve was so highly prized.

He did not produce a great deal of whiskey. Generally, he made just enough to keep his family and friends supplied, with just enough left over to sell to cover his expenses. Obadiah wasn't in it for the money like other distillers in town. The joy was in turning out a superior product. Whiskey was his passion and his art.

Obadiah MacLearnan was a man who was content.

The night air was still, with just a hint of fall. The cabin's newest member, a Highland Collie puppy he had named Porter, was curled up at his feet, fast asleep.

Porter came from a Scots ex-pat who lived a couple of states over. This friend loved both Highland Collies and whiskey in equal amounts. The Scot had suggested a trade, a new puppy for some of Oba's product. Oba laughed and said, "Sure, why not."

Oba enjoyed nights like this, just him and the creatures who belonged there. The forest was quiet and glowed under the light of the waxing gibbous moon.

Glancing down at the front porch floor, he felt, rather than heard, a lean, middle-aged cat come padding up. At night, the cat appeared utterly black. However, in the daylight, he was a deep grey with black whiskers and soft yellow eyes. The cat jumped up and showed no problem walking and sitting on the narrow porch rail.

"Where've you been, you old rascal?" Obadiah asked the young cat. "Out lookin' for trouble, I 'spect."

The Grey Ghost merely raised an eyebrow at this, but his eyes danced with humor, and he purred.

Ghost was the latest cat to call this cabin home. Over the years, Obadiah had raised many animals but never tried to confine them. "I don't 'own' em. They can come and go as they please," he often told people who asked. "Besides, these critters are a lot better company than the two-legged kind," he'd said more than once.

Many of the animals in Obadiah's life would simply show up at the cabin, stay for a spell, and then move on, but the Grey Ghost seemed to be a keeper. He'd found the kitten outside the general store, wet and cold, six years earlier in November. At the time, Ghost could easily fit in the palm of his hand and needed to be bottle-fed. Now, he was full-grown, and one of the best watch-cats Obadiah could ever remember.

Oba and Ghost drew comfort from the dark; they would watch the stars and feel solace.

Ghost's ears twitched without conscious thought, even before Porter's head came up. He looked out at the tree line and let out a very low growl, letting Oba know their privacy was about to be interrupted.

"I hear em," Obadiah confirmed to his friends. "An', I can guess who it is."

"Hey Obadiah, it's Dolion," came a voice from the forest. "Got a minute?"

"Sure. Come on up."

Whereas Obadiah gave little care about appearance, the newcomer showed quite the opposite. He was in his mid-thirties, of average height, with his dark hair slicked back. His hands were pink and soft, displaying a new manicure. A creased pair of jeans with a black pressed oxford shirt and a pair of work boots that never actually saw any hard work completed the picture. Walking alongside was a pure white Persian cat named Lucinda.

"I know why yer here, an' the answer is still no," Obadiah said with no uncertainty.

"Come on, Oba. You make the best whiskey in these parts. Wouldn't you like to share that with a lot more people than those who just live in this valley?"

"Ya don't give a crap bout' quality. If ya did, ya wouldn't have them Boscal boys workin' fer ya. They don't make whiskey; they make paint remover." Then as an afterthought, he added, "You just want all the shine under your control; isn't that so?"

Dolion ignored Oba's insinuation and instead changed the subject. "I hear that McCutcheon's barn burned down last week," he said with feigned sadness. "Thankfully, nobody was hurt, but they lost their still and all their shine. That's the problem with accidents, so damn unpredictable."

While the two men argued, Lucinda sat by Dolion and stared daggers at the grey cat. Ghost tried to ignore her and concentrate on the humans, but he kept an eye on Lucinda. He knew from experience that she was trouble.

Obadiah leaned forward in his chair so that all four legs were on the ground and studied his visitor. "Yeah, accidents are unpredictable," he admitted. "That's why I try to be careful an' plan ahead." Then, reaching down, he brought up a jet-black Mossberg 500 pump 12-gauge shotgun that was practically invisible in the dark.

"I think this visit is over. Git!"

Dolion smiled and turned to leave. Then as an afterthought, he added over his shoulder, "You all are makin' a mistake. I hope you reconsider. Come, Lucinda," he barked. Then, with one last look at Ghost, the Persian turned, flicked her tail, and followed her Person down the mountain.

Obadiah held the shotgun and watched them leave until they were swallowed by the dark. He thought about the veiled threat from Dolion and what he should do about it. *Nothing will be decided tonight,* Oba thought, shaking his head.

"Time for bed, critters," he said to Porter and Ghost. He got up from the chair, stretched, and reached for the door. "You best stay away from that white cat. She's nuthin but trouble," he advised Ghost,

Ghost meowed back, "Way ahead of you on that one." But of course, Oba couldn't speak cat.

Reaching the road at the bottom of the hill, a solitary Cadillac sat idling, a lone driver behind the wheel. Dolion got in while Lucinda jumped into the back seat.

Dolion starred up the mountain toward the cabin. "Arrange an accident. Nothing too dramatic, but something memorable."

Jarred, the driver, nodded dully; he was Dolion's all-around fixer. Jarred wasn't a deep thinker, far from it, but he carried out orders well.

Unbeknownst to everyone in the car, a dark grey cat was sitting in the crook of a tree over the car, and he heard everything.

Joel stopped his story and stared off into space. Belle had been leaning forward and so engaged in the story that she fell forward onto the floor when Joel stopped.

"Then what happened?" the young Protector asked, fidgeting from paw to paw.

"I'm tired. I'll tell you the rest tomorrow," Joel announced. With that, he curled up and closed his eyes.

"But, but…" Belle began when a firm paw patted her on the back. Turning and expecting to see Mittens, she was surprised to see Giblet.

"Leave him be," the tabby cat suggested with sad eyes, clearly moved by what he had heard so far. "Joel has to tell it in his own time."

Belle looked from Giblet to Mittens wondering what she thought. The old Protector just nodded at what Giblet had said. "Go to sleep Belle. Tomorrow will sort itself out."

After their long drive, a good night's sleep was just what the whole family needed; the next thing was to establish a routine for the kids and the animals. Anne and the kids were still asleep when the Woman-Person and Man-Person rose and finished the move-in of everything they hoped would see them through their temporary summer home.

The bedroom door was left open for the cats to come and go as they pleased and explore the house. So, when the Woman-Person called out, *"Breakfast, everyone!"* Anne, the kids, and the pets made their way downstairs to the kitchen.

"Come on, Joel, you might as well come downstairs and eat something," Mittens suggested to the old grey cat. "If you don't, the Woman-Person might think you are sick. You wouldn't enjoy a trip to the vet, would you?"

Joel remained silent but eventually followed the rest of the cats to the kitchen.

Anne and the cats arrived at the kitchen about the same time and stopped in their tracks at what they saw. Except for the relatively modern refrigerator, the rest of the kitchen looked like it stepped out of a 1950 Good Housekeeping article. A half-century-old, large white Magic Chef gas range and oven dominated one wall, while the other two walls held white metal G.E. cabinets. The countertops were wood, except around the sink, where they were white metal with a built-in sink and washboard.

A single window over the sink was framed with red and white plaid curtains, giving a picturesque view of the backyard. An old door with its own window led onto the back porch, and a beautiful wooden table, large enough to seat eight people, was in the middle of the kitchen.

What wasn't present in the kitchen was one single labor-saving appliance. There wasn't a dishwasher, microwave oven, or even electric can opener to be found. However, there was a coffee percolator on the stove that looked like it came from the 1950s.

"This looks just like my grandparent's kitchen," Anne said aloud to anyone listening.

"I know. Isn't it great?" the woman person responded as she explored the cabinets and drawers.

"Yeah. It looks like the kids will learn how to hand wash dishes," the Man-Person said with a smile while examining the old coffee pot, wondering how to make it work.

Fortunately, the family had packed a few groceries, and Marie had stocked the refrigerator with some milk, eggs, and butter before the family had arrived, so breakfast could commence. Iko got her bowl of kibble, the cats got their morning dry food, and the kids got their cereal. The adults sat and read their phones or tablets and tried their first cup of coffee from a vintage coffee percolator when a knock at the front door broke the silence.

"I'll get it," the Man-Person volunteered.

He returned to the kitchen with their early arrival. Iko and three cats looked at the visitor while Giblet kept eating. Marie, the woman who had dropped off the key last night, was back with another set of keys and a list of phone numbers for businesses in town that the family might find helpful.

Seeing all the animals in the kitchen, Marie commented, "Uncle Obadiah would be thrilled so many critters are in this old house again," she said as she watched the cats have breakfast. Her gaze settled on Joel, who did his best to ignore her. "I said it before, but that cat looks just like the one my Uncle used to have."

Joel felt Marie's eyes upon him. When he could no longer stand the scrutiny, he stopped eating and stared back, his face displaying a mixture of sadness and guilt. When his emotions became overwhelming, he began to shake and took off for the stairs and the safety of the bedroom.

After a moment, Anne asked, "What happened to your uncle?"

"I don't know. It was right before Thanksgiving, and I wasn't home from my senior year in college. The authorities called me when they couldn't find Uncle Oba. I came home and went straight to his cabin to find it still full of things, but he was nowhere to be found. His dog,

Porter, was there and looked like he hadn't been fed in a couple of days, so I took Porter home with me and reported Uncle Oba missing."

"Did the police investigate?" the Man-Person asked.

"The police conducted a halfhearted investigation but didn't find evidence of foul play or my uncle. They interviewed people in town who said he had been seen around town right before Thanksgiving but that they hadn't seen him recently. Finally, after a month of doing basically nothing, the police chief said that Oba probably died somewhere on the mountain, and it was more than likely an accident."

"Did they use tracking dogs to try to find him?" Anne asked, always a detective at heart.

"I don't think so. The cabin wasn't disturbed, and no signs of a struggle were ever found. They think he fell in a ravine on the mountain or had an accident. I told them that Oba knew that mountain like the back of his hand; he wouldn't walk into a ravine. So their theory didn't make any sense."

"I am sorry for your loss," The Woman-Person said compassionately.

While the people continued to chat, Mittens motioned for Belle and Giblet to follow her back to the bedroom.

Mittens again found Joel in the carrier, with his back to the door.

"Come on out, Joel. It's time you finished your story," she purred compassionately.

Giblet, who had kept quiet during Joel's story last night, softly meowed encouragement. "You helped me with my pain and guilt about my brother. It helped me to get it out. You've kept it inside long enough."

Joel turned around and came to the door of the carrier. He began his story again with a look on his face that was 50 percent guilt and 50 percent resignation.

CHAPTER V

The Plan

"Remember," he said while pointing his finger at the fixer's chest, "All I want is a broken leg or arm...."

Three Days Before Thanksgiving, Ten Years Before.

Cold frosty mornings with only a few leaves left on the trees, it was Thanksgiving week in Busby, West Virginia, and the whole town was excited. The townspeople were looking forward to the holiday and the annual Turkey-Day high school football game between the Busby Central High Comets and their rivals from the next county, the White Mountain High School Panthers. The Turkey-Day match had been going on since the turn of the century and was the years' high point for both communities.

The original trophy was a jug of locally produced whiskey for the winning team provided by a local distiller. Obadiah's family had provided much of the trophy whiskey in the old days. Even then, Oba's family recipe was coveted, and legend said both teams played their hearts out for that particular prize.

Things changed, of course, when church groups in both towns decided it was sinful to provide whiskey to a group of fifteen, sixteen, and seventeen-year-old boys so they could get drunk. So nowadays, the prize was an 'empty' whiskey jug with a sculpted football player affixed to the top. People said the award was still coveted as a symbol of school pride, just not enjoyed quite as much.

The game location alternated each year between the towns, and it was Busby's turn to host this year. The resulting enthusiasm for the big game ensured there wouldn't be a parking spot available within several miles of the school.

Unfortunately, the Comets had lost the last two years, and the trophy had stayed with the White Mountain High School team. However, the Comets had a real shot at winning this year's game because of their stellar lineup. *"Finally, the trophy will come home to Busby,"* people said as they passed each other in the streets.

Last-minute preparations were underway throughout the community; final bets were placed on the game, turkeys were picked up at the butcher store for after-game dinners, and last-minute pie ingredients were grabbed at the local market. There wasn't a single can of pumpkin filling available anywhere in the valley; you were out of luck if you couldn't prepare your own pumpkin pie filling from scratch.

Obadiah was also very busy. He had a list of family and friends that were expecting some of his famous whiskey to —hopefully— celebrate a Busby Comets win. In fact, a number of his customers were former Comet players from years before who fondly remembered Oba's whiskey after their team's win.

Oba left his cabin early that morning with Ghost in tow and hiked up the hill to the abandoned coal mine on his property, home of the MacLearnan family distillery. "Come on, you old rascal," Oba called to Ghost after putting on his coat.

As far as he could tell, nobody alive knew where the mine was. The mine was started in the early 1800s and was quickly forgotten when the amount of coal it produced was too small to continue the investment. After the mine closed, the original owner sold the property to Oba's great grandfather and moved out of state. That was when the mine began its second existence as the production home of the best small-batch whiskey in West Virginia.

Setting a brisk pace for someone his age, Oba hiked up the mountainside with Ghost. The grey cat would leap-frog ahead and stop to listen. Then, as Oba passed, he would repeat the maneuver, ensuring they were alone.

About halfway up the mountain, the ground pitched down into an oval-shaped cleft in the terrain. It was bigger than a sinkhole and looked to be formed when the mountain was created. It was situated in such a way that it was not readily visible unless you stood right over it and looked down.

When you did look down into the gap, all you would see was more forest floor, a few scrub trees, and a boulder resting near the top of the oval. The rock was big, about the size of a minivan, with patches of lichen; it looked like it had always been there. The entrance to the mine was behind the boulder, with the actual opening covered by decades of plant growth. As a result, you could literally stand a dozen feet from the mine entrance and not even know it was there.

Why anyone would pick this hidden, almost inaccessible spot to have a coal mine was explained when they realized the mine was actually a small, naturally formed cave. That made starting the original mine much more practical. So even though the mine didn't pan out, the clandestine location made perfect sense for making shine.

Ghost leaped up and scaled the boulder. Sitting like a statue, his eyes and ears darted left and right, trying to pick up any unnatural movement or sound. Finally, after half a minute, he gave a low rumbling meow, letting Oba know they were not followed. These security measures had increased since Dolion had developed an interest in acquiring Oba's still for himself.

An adult had to bend over to get through the mine entrance, but they could straighten up once inside. Long ago, one of Oba's ancestors had dug out more of the mine ceiling so you could stand upright and be comfortable while working, a distinct advantage when you spent hours distilling a batch of whiskey.

The first thing was to light several kerosene hurricane lamps. Oba considered switching to battery-powered lights a while back, and while that might have had advantages, keeping any battery charged up would have been a challenge. Besides, the old lamps cast a comfortable yellow glow that would have been very familiar to his ancestors; it made Oba feel like he was carrying on a tradition in his whiskey making.

The original claustrophobic mine tunnel had been enlarged considerably. Several additional rooms connecting to the main chamber were dug out over the years to provide enough working area. Past the main chamber and deeper into the mine, the contours of the walls and ceiling returned to the way they were initially dug, about forty-four inches high by about forty-eight inches wide. Oba and Ghost never ventured into these areas because all the distilling and other activity occurred near the front of the mine. Besides, a hundred feet up the mine shaft, a sudden drop-off went down several stories.

The antique copper still sat in the main chamber and took up much of the space. On it, a whimsical sign was painted by Oba a few years before:

MacLearnan Distillery—Est. 1885— Obadiah & Ghost, Proprietors.

The still was tall, and the Onion-Head at the top almost brushed the ceiling of the mine. The boiler, or pot as it's known, had been patched a few times over the years and was still in good shape. The copper tubing showed the passage of time with a green hue of oxidation. Yet, despite its age and appearance, the Still was a thing of beauty to the man and his cat.

The Still sat over a modern propane burner connected to a white LP gas tank. The wood firebox that had once supported the still had been removed when Oba took over the family business. The LP gas was one concession to modern technology; it didn't smoke, and it provided a continuous regulated flame that kept the distillation at a constant even flow, about two to three drops per second. The collection cup was a five-gallon crockery jug that was older than Oba. Overall, it took about fifteen hours to make a three-and-a-half-gallon batch of new whiskey, also known as White-Dog, that had a barrel entry of 150-proof.

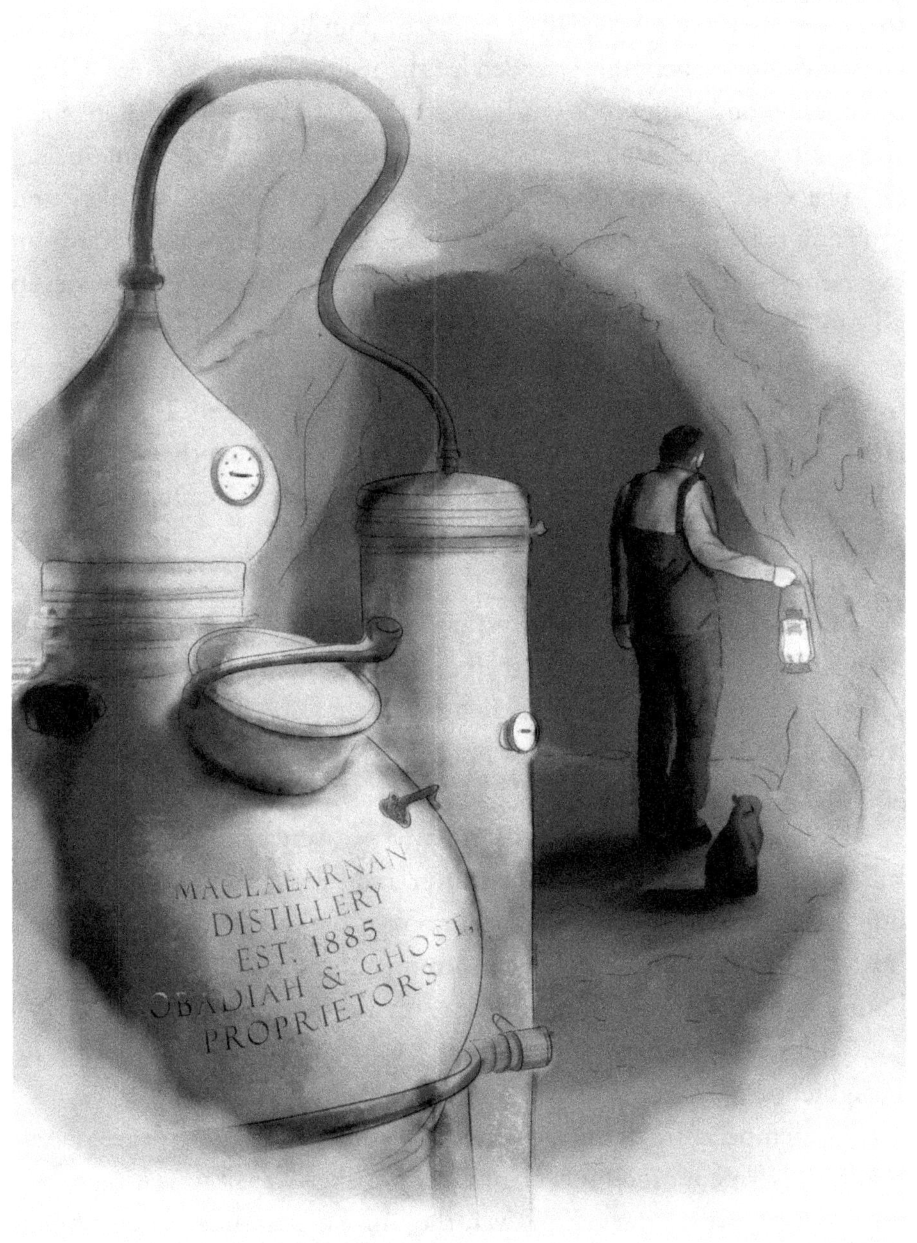

MACLAEARNAN
DISTILLERY
EST. 1885
OBADIAH & GHOST,
PROPRIETORS

After ensuring everything was in order outside, Ghost joined Oba in the mine. He followed as Oba moved from the central part of the mine to an antechamber on the left. The mash room held several large bags of corn and a few other grains needed for the recipe. The sacks were stacked on an old wood pallet to keep them off the dirt floor. In addition, there was some yeast in a sealed glass jar and several plastic water containers.

The water was the easiest ingredient to obtain for the whiskey and probably the most important. Just outside the mine entrance, less than one hundred yards away, an active spring produced the sweetest water in all Appalachian mountains. It had a perfect balance with just the right amount of minerals to promote yeast growth but not so many minerals to affect the finished product's taste. According to legend, Busby always had excellent water, which is why the town was founded there.

Several mice scattered when Ghost and his Person came in. "Rrrowwllrrr—I'm keeping an eye on you," Ghost said to the retreating mice.

Besides being an excellent watch cat, Ghost kept the local rodent population in check. He knew the grains were enticing for the mice who called the mine home, so he tolerated a little thievery. However, too many free meals, and he would have to put his paw down. The mice knew this and didn't press their luck.

Three glass jugs were in the room; two were empty, but one was full of fermenting mash. Oba bent over and peered in the jug. Tiny air bubbles were still collecting in the airlock at the top, so the mash wasn't ready. When the yeast finished consuming all the sugar in the mash, the bubbles would stop, and it would be ready for the still.

"At least another day for the mash," Oba announced to Ghost as he straightened up.

The temperature in the mine was an almost constant 57 degrees. As a result, the fermentation process for Oba's whiskey was slow, lasting a little more than fourteen days. However, the unrushed approach contributed to the wonderfully smooth whiskey.

"Come along, you old rascal," Oba said to Ghost as he went into another room in the mine. Making good whiskey was a ziggurat with many steps and more than a few pitfalls to one's goal.

Off to the right was another chamber that had been enlarged over the years. Originally, the space might have been where the miners had lunch, but today it was the aging room. There were dozens of five-gallon white oak barrels on ricks lining the chamber wall, aging peacefully. A handwritten date on the end of each barrel told Oba when the whiskey had been put down to age.

Whiskey can be aged for any number of years. Three years is the minimum, while scotch can be over fifty. The span of years contributes to both coloring the whiskey and mellowing it. Oba aged his whiskey a minimum of ten years—however, a half dozen barrels approached twenty-five years or older. The oldest was labeled—My Funeral Wake, Marie's Graduation Party (for his niece), and the last was labeled; For fun.

A standard whiskey barrel is fifty-three gallons, but Oba had a cooper who lived in the Ozarks of Missouri who made smaller barrels for him in return for keeping the cooper supplied with a steady stream of the finished product.

An old handmade wooden table was where Oba tapped the barrels and filled the two different-sized bottles his whiskey came in; pints and fifths. The plain glass bottles came to his house in Busby from a canning supply store, along with a bag of cork stoppers to seal the bottles. Originally, Oba dipped the filled bottles in sealing wax before delivering them. However, his customers let him know that the whiskey was often opened and drank almost as soon as they received the delivery. Since the whiskey wouldn't stay on a shelf for long, he stopped the practice.

"It looks good in here," Oba said, looking down at Ghost.

Any serious whiskey distiller can tell you the three things that will make a good whiskey: water, grains, and aging. It was the combination of these ingredients, tweaked and refined over hundreds of batches and in exact proportions, that gave the MacLearnan whiskey its exceptional taste. The family called the process the recipe, and it has been passed down, parent to sibling, for over a hundred-and-twenty-five years.

The original recipe was written down by Oba's ancestor with a quill pen on old-fashioned, high-quality plain cream paper with a nice thick weight. Today, the recipe was available only in two places: Oba's head and the original document.

Many people confuse bourbon and whiskey, thinking they are the same thing. And while they share many similarities, Oba prided himself as a whiskey distiller and would launch into a recitation if questioned.

"The difference between bourbon and whiskey is the make-up of the grains in the mash," Oba would lecture. "The mash has to be 51 percent or more corn to be called bourbon. On the other hand, whiskey can be made from a variety of grains, includin' corn, rye, barley, and/or wheat, to name a few. My mash has corn and a selection of other grains in precise proportions. My ancestors trialed for years until they came up with a recipe that produces our signature product.

Another issue in makin' good whiskey is the water. You must be sure that the raw whiskey and water are combined at the same temperatures. It's a greenhorn mistake to add water that is too cold or too hot, an' the finished whiskey will always show the mistake."

Most people came away from Oba's whiskey lectures with more distilling facts than they could hope to remember. However, many were happy to listen because the reward usually was a pint of the special recipe

Oba went over to some bottles he had filled earlier in the week. The amber liquid danced in the lamp light and seemed to give off a soft glow on its own. Oba smiled and looked down at Ghost, "I think these will do fine." Ghost meowed in agreement.

Traditional moonshine whiskey is either clear or very lightly colored, but Oba's product was the color of Bourbon, a light chestnut brown; Bourbon and whiskey get their color and some of their distinctive flavors from aging in charred barrels. First, the whiskey producer would fire the inside of the barrel for less than a minute, creating a thin layer of charred wood. Then, as the 150-proof White Dog whiskey aged in outdoor rickhouses, temperature changes would swell and contract the barrels, forcing the whiskey into and out of the charred walls. It is this back-and-forth that gives the whiskey or bourbon its distinctive color and taste.

Oba fired his barrels, but before he set the barrel head in the chime and hammered it down with a mallet, he would add a dozen staves from old barrels he used for prior distillations. The mine was generally the same temperature year-round, limiting the barrels' expansion and contraction. The extra charred staves made up for the consistent air temperature. In fact, Oba would tell you that the easy, slow aging made his whiskey taste better.

Before Oba would pour the newly distilled White-Dog into the barrels, he would wash the inside of each barrel with one cup of Graham's Ten-Year Tawny Port. A case of the wine was kept in the aging room, next to new barrels he'd received last month.

Oba fell in love with the layered, complex dessert wine when he visited the Douro Valley as a young man of twenty, tramping across Europe. The future distiller watched port wine being made and sampled some of the finest ports in the world. While he would always love his whiskey, Oba would never turn down an after-dinner port.

The addition of the fortified wine was Oba's contribution to the old family recipe. It made the distillation truly his and made his whiskey the most unique and sought-after moonshine in West Virginia and perhaps the country.

Ghost meowed that everything looked in order, and Oba smiled. Then, filling a box with a dozen bottles, he turned to his cat and said, "These look good. Let's git. We got deliveries to make before the big game."

Oba began extinguishing the lamps and headed toward the exit with Ghost in tow. Before long, they were down the mountain and in Busby, making their deliveries. Each person was delighted to get their order before the big game and Thanksgiving.

Pretty soon, Oba had distributed all his whiskey and told Ghost, "I'm heading back to the cabin. Are you comin' with me?"

Since he was in town, Ghost wanted to go to the Butcher Shop and see if he could get any free handouts. He meowed once to Oba and then headed back toward Main Street.

"Be good, you old rascal," Oba called after him and smiled.

In another part of town, Dolion was giving orders to his fixer.

"I saw Obadiah making deliveries this morning. I know for a fact that he is going to get a few more orders while he is in town." The fixer stared at his boss with a vacant look on his face.

Ignoring the puzzlement on his subordinate face, he went on, "When he goes back to his still for more whiskey, you and I will tail him. Today we will find out where his still is. Then, on his way back, he will have his accident."

Jarred nodded dully but otherwise didn't react to the instructions.

"Remember," Dolion said while pointing his finger at the fixer's chest, "All I want is a broken leg or arm. I want the fool to work for us. We can make a fortune off of his shine."

"What about his cat warning him?" Jarred mumbled.

Dolion was impressed that his fixer could come up with a legitimate question like that. Perhaps he'd underestimated him? "Lucinda is going to distract his cat so we can follow unobserved."

"Unob-what?" Jarred mumbled.

Dolion sighed and shook his head. No, he hadn't overestimated him.

Joel stopped his story when they all heard the front door slamming. Jumping to the window, Belle watched the Man-Person and Woman-Person leaving for the day. They headed up the street holding hands.

"It's just the Man and Woman going," she reported to the rest of the cats from the windowsill. Then, jumping down, she rejoined the group, expecting to hear the rest of the story. Instead, Joel had laid his head down and closed his eyes.

"I think he is tired. Let's give him a rest, and he can finish later," Mittens purred wisely. "Belle, want to go explore our new home?" the Maine Coon asked her apprentice.

Belle nodded her head enthusiastically and followed Mittens to the door.

"I will stay with Joel," Giblet meowed. "I don't think he should be alone."

That's a good idea," Mittens agreed as she joined Belle at the bedroom door.

Giblet got up, stretched, and turned around three times before settling back down next to Joel. He saw that Joel was asleep and was having a bad dream. Reaching out with his paw, he patted Joel compassionately.

"The guilt we carry with us is the heaviest burden," Giblet purred knowingly before closing his eyes.

CHAPTER VI

The Warning

"Dinna fash yersel, ye can't fool this hooter, young
lassie. Ah smelled four different cats last night,"
Porter said, raising his nose in the air. "Who ar' ye?"

9:00 A.M., Eastern Cat Time.

Mittens explored the house with Belle in the lead. They inspected every room, including the attic. It was full of old furniture, boxes, and several steamer trunks. Everything was covered with a thick coating of dust, and cobwebs hung in the corners. The cellar contained the boiler for the radiators, a water heater that looked older than Joel, and some steps that led up to a pair of doors going outside.

However, the strangest discovery of all was a small dog door built into one of the old cellar windows. It was only accessible by leaping onto one shelf and then crossing over to another by the windows.

"It goes out to the back yard," Belle reported after poking her head out the old but still working flap. "But I don't understand how a dog could use this. No dog could get up on this shelf."

"This house had a cat at some time in the past," Mittens guessed correctly. "These People put this door in so their cat could go outside whenever they wanted. We will put their ingenuity to good use and use this door for patrols, even if this is a temporary neighborhood for us."

First, Belle, then Mittens went through the flap and found themselves standing in a long, rectangular backyard with a short picket fence around the perimeter.

"Let's go," Mittens purred and headed off.

The two cats easily got over the back fence and made their way to the front of the house.

"Which way?" Belle asked.

"Let's go right," was the answer from Mittens.

"Any reason?"

"Not a darn one," came the Protector's reply.

Both cats moved up the street, following the sidewalk. Both agreed that the little town was picturesque, with an old-fashioned, comfortable feel about it. The houses were mostly one and two-story white clapboard with large front porches and neatly tended yards. And, more than a few places had the obligatory white picket wood fence that made them look like a Norman Rockwell painting.

A couple of houses up, they saw a small, one-story home with beautiful gardens and an old, rather furry dog lying on the porch.

The dog watched them walk past and lifted his head to sniff the air. Then, satisfied, he woofed a greeting to the two cats on the sidewalk, causing them to stop.

"Awright thare, yer th' twa cats unmoved in lest night," he said with a thick, unknown brogue.

Both cats looked at the dog and then at each other. Finally, Belle whispered to Mittens, "Do you know what that dog is saying?"

"Unless I miss my guess, our furry friend there is Scottish," Mittens told Belle. "Where are you from?" she meowed, intrigued by the large dog's accent.

"A'm fae th' hielands of' Scootlund," he woofed. "Ye kin ca' me, Porter."

"How did you know we just moved in?" Belle questioned, following the conversation with difficulty.

"Ah was wit' mah Person last night when we visited. Ah smelled ye," Porter announced.

"But you never saw us," Belle challenged. "We were in our carriers."

"Dinna fash yersel wee barin, ye can't fool this hooter. Ah smelled four different cats last night, an ye be twa of them," Porter said, raising his nose in the air. "Who ar' ye?"

"I'm Belle, and this is Mittens," Belle said and motioned with her paw. "We are Protectors."

"Ah dinnae ken whit Protector is, but ah tell ye, ah smelled somthin' kenspeckle las' night," he woofed.

"Kenspeckle?" Belle asked, turning her head to the side.

"Ita' means familiar. I smelled one o' you before. Where ye from?"

"We're from Torrington. It's a town in Connecticut, up north," Belle added for good measure.

"Whit's a Protector?" Porter woofed.

"It's an ancient society of cats who have pledged to help mankind and protect People," Belle said proudly.

"Mittens," Belle gestured with her paw, "is my teacher. She and her family have been Protectors for hundreds of years." Mittens smiled down at Belle, seeing the genuine pride in her pupil.

Porter went on, "Now tha ye mention it, I remember a cat from long ago that helped and took care of ma first owner. Ah dinnae ken the name Protector though. I just called em Ghost".

Mittens had been half-listening to Belle and half-planning the rest of their patrol until Porter mentioned the name Ghost. Immediately, all other concerns were filed away, and her whole attention was focused on the dog. Likewise, Belle gave a start at hearing Joel Grey's nom de plume.

"You wouldn't have known a Person named Obadiah, would you?" Mittens asked, observing the dog.

"Aye, certainly dae ken him. He was my first gaffer years ago. Howfur did ye come by that name?"

"Obadiah raised our friend also," Belle piped up.

Interested, the old Highland Collie rose slowly from the porch and walked over to Belle and Mittens. "That kenspeckle cat ah smelled, ah knew ah recognized it— Whit's yer' mukker's name?"

"We call him Joel Grey, but you may know him as the Grey Ghost," Mittens meowed, watching for a reaction.

"Jings! Ghost ye say? That's a name ah hadn't heard in a long time. He disappeared th' identical time Obadiah gone missin'," Porter woofed sadly.

"Can you tell us what happened that day he went missing?" Mittens meowed.

"Ah, ye ken. Ah was a wee pup when Obadiah left tae go tae th' mine. He 'n' came back 'n' left a'gin. Oba dinna shut the door, an ah followed 'em. After what happened, I came back an ah wus alone for almost two days, 'til Marie came round 'n' rescued me. I hae bin wi' her ever since."

"When your Person went to the mine, was Joel…er, I mean Ghost with him?" Belle asked.

"The first time they gone tae th' mine, Ghost wis wi' him. When Oba wenna' back tae th' mine, Ghost was nae where ta be foond."

"Why didn't Ghost go with Oba the second time," Mittens asked, leaning forward.

"Ah dinnae ken. Oba looked for him, a couldna' find em, so ye went alone." Then, after a moment, Porter added, "But Oba dinnae make it tae the mine, he came back hame."

"Can you excuse us a moment," Mittens asked the Highlander. Porter nodded his head.

Motioning to Belle to follow, the two cats walked a few feet away and discussed what they had learned.

"So, what do you think?" Belle asked in a hushed tone.

"I'm not sure. Joel is certainly blaming himself for whatever happened to Obadiah. Porter said he didn't make it to the mine but instead came back home," Mittens said, deep in thought.

"Do you think Porter telling him it wasn't his fault will help Joel?"

Mittens nodded and said, "It might. I have an idea." They walked back to the Highlander, and Mittens smiled at the old dog, "Porter, we have a favor to ask you…."

The Woman-Person and Man-Person returned to the house a little after five; both were happy with their first day but eager to relax after a long day. In the man's arms was a small, modern coffee maker for the kitchen. Unfortunately, the Man-Person's first foray into vintage coffee making was not a success.

Like in Torrington, Giblet and Belle joined them for cocktail hour, eager for a handout of whatever snacks they were eating. Anne also joined them for a glass of wine before dinner.

"I met my students for the summer," the Woman-Person stated, running her finger up and down the stem of the wine glass she had just poured.

"How do they look?" Anne asked while rubbing Giblet between the ears as he purred.

"They seem bright and inquisitive," she happily reported. "Summer class students usually fall into one of two categories; those who didn't do well and have to retake the class or those students who are motivated and want to get a jump on the coursework."

"That's true," the Man-Person said as he poured his martini into a plain glass. He'd brought his favorite gin and vermouth from Connecticut but left his "new" special martini glass home. Looking at the plain glass, he sighed deeply, "Oh well. Allowances must be made."

"These students seem like they want to be in class," the woman speculated. "I think it is going to be a fun class."

Belle had jumped onto the counter but stayed away from the martini. Knocking it over once had been enough for any cat. So, she contented herself with a few scratches from the Man-Person under her chin and between the ears.

Anne and the two Professors retired to the front porch to have their cocktails and enjoy the late afternoon. Belle and Giblet were stopped by the screen door. However, both sat and listened to the People's conversation.

"I had an interesting visit from the police chief while I was in the library doing research," the Man-Person said conversationally. "He told me to be careful asking people too many questions about moonshining and bootlegging, especially since I was a Yankee."

"You're kidding, right?" the Woman-Person asked.

"Not really," he said. "The police chief said, and I quote: 'Some people here don't cotton to strangers sticking their nose in other people's business.'"

"Is that going to affect your research?" Anne asked"

"I hope not. Jarred, the chief, said he would take me around if I wanted to talk to people, but first, he wanted to introduce me."

At the mention of Jarred's name, Belle reached over and tapped Giblet on the shoulder. "Stop grooming and listen. This is important."

"Why?" Giblet asked.

"Jarred was in Joel's story last night," Belle whisper-purred.

"The funny thing," the Man-Person went on, "is how he knew about my research topic. Other than the college and the young woman who rented us this house, I don't think I told anyone about what I was doing."

"This is a small town, and we are strangers. He probably wondered who we were and asked questions," the Woman-Person observed shrewdly. "In a small town like this, somebody with a new hairstyle would be front-page news."

"How true," Anne said laughing, and the Man-Person smiled.

Belle, Mittens, and Giblet had a meeting upstairs while the People prepared dinner.

"Did you get any more out of Joel?" Mittens questioned.

"No. Joel slept most of the day and just woke up a little while ago," Giblet relayed. "He still hasn't left his carrier."

"FURR-BALLS…DINNER!"

All three cats turned their heads when the Woman-Person's voice echoed up from the first floor.

"Dinner. FINALLY!" Giblet said and started for the door, only to stop and look behind him. Belle and Mittens hadn't moved. Instead, they were looking at Joel, who had not emerged from the carrier.

"Dinner time Joel," Belle said with her usual happy voice, but Joel seemed to ignore her.

"Joel, either you come to dinner, or the Woman-Person is going to come up here and see what's wrong," Mittens said to the reluctant grey cat.

With no reasonable alternative at paw, Joel slowly got up and followed the rest of the cats out the bedroom door in silence. Soon, all four cats were in the kitchen and having dinner while the family had theirs.

After dinner, the Woman person suggested that everyone sit outside and enjoy the evening. Soon, everyone was on the porch. The grown-ups enjoyed coffee from the new appliance, and the Children were given ice cream.

"You know, I could get used to this," The Man-Person said from the rocking chair he claimed.

"I don't think you would be happy, living so far away from the liquor store that sold your special gin and French vermouth," the Woman-Person teased.

After dinner, Joel tried to go back upstairs but was convinced to hang out in the front room and watch the family through the screen door. But, of course, convinced implied he had an alternative, Iko had blocked the stairs, and Mittens, Giblet, and Belle somewhat dragged him into the front room.

"Hello, neighbors," a friendly and easygoing voice called out from the sidewalk. Everyone looked down to see a tall, middle-aged man coming up the walk to the front porch.

The man had slicked-back hair and bright white teeth. He was wearing pressed Dockers with a distinct crease running down each leg, an oxford shirt that looked freshly ironed, and a pair of casual shoes that looked expensive and like they had never been outside.

"You must be the Macgregor family," he said with a smile.

The stranger stopped at the steps to the front porch and was soon joined by a large, pure white Persian cat that rubbed against his legs. "I'm the mayor of this little town, but everybody around here calls me Dolion." Then looking down, he added, "And this is my cat, Lucinda."

After a moment, the white Persian cat sat down and fixed her gaze. She didn't look at the People on the porch but rather at the animals inside the house. Her gaze shifted from one cat to another, her own private calculus going on in her head. Then her eyes settled on Joel, and a scowl spread across her face.

Mittens calmly returned the white cat's gaze, not liking what she saw.

Belle and Giblet turned and looked at Joel, worried he would run upstairs as soon as Dolion had mentioned his name. However, Joel didn't leave; he stared hard at the visitors.

"Joel, you're shaking," Belle meowed softly, thinking he was afraid. She added, "It will be all right."

'No, he's not afraid," Mittens purred, glancing at Joel and then turning back to Lucinda. "That's pure rage."

The Man-Person Got up, came down the stairs, and offered his hand to their visitor, "I'm Russell. Pleased to meet you. Come up and have a cup of coffee with us." The mayor followed, but his cat stayed on the sidewalk, staring at Joel.

After they were all seated, introductions were made. "Shirley. She is working at the college this summer while I do my research," the Man-Person said, motioning to the Woman-Person, who had just handed him a cup of coffee. "And this Anne Gaumont," he said, finishing introductions. "She is our adopted grandmother for the family."

Anne smiled and offered her hand to Dolion. "Nice to meet you, Mr. Mayor," she acknowledged, noticing with her detective's eye for detail that the man's hands were pink and soft, with manicured nails. Not one for physical labor, she thought.

"Dolion. Everyone calls me Dolion," he said with an easygoing smile. "How did you get to become an 'adopted' grandma?" he asked, blowing a little on the coffee to cool it.

"That all came about when this lovely family moved next door. My late husband and I never had kids, so this is a lot of fun for me."

"Before she retired, Anne was Senior Detective Gaumont of the Torrington Police Department," Shirley added.

Dolion continued smiling, but Mittens and Belle caught a very subtle change in his demeanor when the word "Detective" was announced. Only a Protector or a well-trained Person would notice such a subtle change. Belle glanced at Anne and knew she saw it to.

Dolion responded jokingly, "Detective. Well, I better behave myself," he said with a chuckle.

"I'm enjoying the retired life too much to go back to work," Anne said with her matching smile. "I did have the opportunity to work with your state patrol on a couple of cases over the years. They're a great group, a real credit to the state," she praised.

"Dolion, I have a quick question," the Man-Person asked, changing the subject. "Why did the police chief warn me about asking questions for my research? After all, it's hardly a secret that this area used to be the center for whiskey production in the 1800s and through Prohibition?"

While their father was speaking, Cassidy and Christopher went down the steps to the front yard to greet the Mayor's cat.

"Aw hell, Jarred shouldn't have told you that. I'll speak to him in the morning," Dolion said casually. "People around here are just reserved. I'm sure he just wanted to head off any misunderstanding. After all, we wouldn't want you to think the people of Busby are rude. I think that—" The mayor never got to finish what he was saying because

Lucinda let out a loud hiss and swatted at Christopher's outstretched hand with her claws.

A growl came out of Mittens and Iko simultaneously from inside the house, but the loudest howl of protest came from Joel; he hit the screen door with his body, trying to get through. Both Mittens and Belle looked at Joel pressed against the screen and heard his warning to the white Persian – *"Don't you dare harm those Children, or you will be dealin' with me!"*

"Lucinda, STOP," Dolion scolded. Then to the parents, "I'm sure she just got spooked because she doesn't know you," he said with an apology. "She's getting cranky in her old age."

Looking at the Boy, Dolion asked, "Did she get you?"

Christopher shook his head, and then the Mom-Person called the children back to the porch, "I think everyone is tired after their first day here. It's bedtime for these two."

"And I have to be going also. Busy day tomorrow," the mayor replied. "Be sure to ask me if you need anything for your research."

The Man-Person thanked Dolion for stopping by and promised he would come to him if he needed anything. Then the parents and the kids went into the house. Giblet and Iko followed them upstairs for bedtime.

Soon it was just Anne alone on the porch with the night. Then, after a minute, she got up, stretched, and let Belle, Mittens, and Joel out onto the porch with her.

Belle jumped on Anne's lap while Mittens and Joel listened to the sounds of the night.

"That's him and his cat," Mittens observed, looking into the night.

"Yup, that's him," Joel confirmed sadly.

"I don't like him, even if I didn't know the story," Belle announced.

Anne was content to listen to the cats. Her cop-senses told her that Dolion was dirty, but of what?

"It wasn't your fault, Joel, and I have proof," Mittens confided.

"What proof?"

"The proof will be here in a little while. First, we have to wait for the People to fall asleep," Belle said.

"Mittens, what is going on?" Anne finally asked.

"Joel was born and grew up here," Mittens said. "His first owner, Obadiah, was killed by Dolion and we're gonna prove it," the Protector announced.

Sitting there in the dark, Anne sighed. *So much for retirement.*

"Just what in the Sam Hill do you think you were doing with stupid little warning to a college professor?" a very angry Dolion questioned the police chief over the phone. "For Christ's sake, this isn't a rival gang trying to move in on our operation. It's an egghead writing a book. And, you've gone and made him suspicious of our town."

The silence from the other end of the phone was deafening.

"Well, I'm waiting."

"I jus' didn't want him messin' with our business or looking into Obadiah," Jarred mumbled into the receiver. "He's stayin' in Obadiah's old house, doggone it. What if he starts asking questions about him?"

"He doesn't know Obadiah from Adam," the mayor said confidently. "I checked him out as soon as you opened your stupid mouth with your warning. He's a tenured professor from Torrington College on a three-month research sabbatical with a research grant for a book on the history of moonshine."

"What's a 'stubbitcal'?" Jarred asked his boss.

"Never mind," Dolion answered. "Just leave the egghead alone and don't go making any more waves." Dolion decided not to mention that Macgregor's nanny/grandma was a retired detective. Better not to crowd Jarred's head with too much information.

"I just thought…"

"Don't think. You're not good at it. Just polish your pretty badge and do what I tell you." And with that, Dolion put the phone down.

Jarred looked at the phone that sat on his desk. *One of these days, Dolion. One of these days,* he thought.

Lucinda was curled up in her house with Dolion, thinking about Ghost and the other cats who'd returned to Busby with him. They represented a problem for her and her owner. A problem that she would have to deal with.

She was sure these cats would start sticking their noses into Dolion's business sooner or later because of what Ghost would tell them. She was also confident she could handle most of the cats, but the large Maine Coon gave her pause.

"That Maine Coon is a Protector, I'm sure of it," she thought to herself. Lucinda was under no illusion about a Protector's skills and ability, having experienced them before. *"I can handle Ghost and the other two cats, but that Protector will be tricky."*

She also knew that Ghost could lead them to Obadiah's old still and the recipe for his moonshine, something Dolion had been after for over ten years.

"I'm going to keep an eye on that clowder. And, when they go to the still, I will be ready."

CHAPTER VII

Clues Discovered

"We're doomed," Giblet added…

11:00 P.M.–
The Full Mouse Hunting Moon of June.

The family was fast asleep, and cats had assembled along with Anne on the front porch. They were all waiting on the visitor that Belle and Mittens promised, with varying degrees of interest. Ranging from eager anticipation for Belle and Mittens to curiosity from Giblet, and finally, dread embodied on Joel's face.

Only crickets and the growl of a couple of air-conditioners broke the silence for everyone gathered. Busby was the kind of town that mostly rolled up the sidewalks after about nine-thirty at night, with one, or rather, two exceptions. Those exceptions were one spit-and-sawdust bar called The Rose and one flashy-trash bar called Dolion's Place. Both bars were on the southern end of town and couldn't have been more different.

The Rose was the oldest bar in Busby and perhaps in all of Western Virginia. It could trace its roots back to the pre-Civil War when the Rose family decided they needed to generate extra income. Great, great grandmother Mary Rose MacLearnan began selling her special recipe whiskey out of the livery stable they owned at the cost of a silver half-dime per shot. The first customers of Rose's establishment were destined to enjoy their whiskey with the smell of sweaty horses and fresh manure. Gradually, the horses were relocated because Mary Rose decided the horses deserved better company with a higher level of personal hygiene.

Legend says that Busby wasn't burned to the ground by either the Confederacy or the Union during the War because Mary Rose provided free whiskey to whoever was occupying the town at that time.

The bar top at the Rose had so many initials carved into it by people over the years you couldn't find an unscored spot. The most famous initials (R.E.L) were carved into the bar before the Confederacy was forced out of West Virginia. To this day, General Lee's initials are preserved on the bar top under a sheet of glass.

The Rose's wasn't glamorous, not by a long shot. It consisted of a long bar with beer taps on the front and back of the bar. Liquor bottles were placed wherever they were handy to grab, and only three barstools matched each other. The tables on the floor had mismatched chairs and needed shims so they wouldn't wobble. The centerpiece of the back bar was added in the early nineteen hundreds and was a large mirror with a beautiful red rose painted on it.

Basic pub fare was served at the Rose, with one exception. They had some of the best barbecue in the state of West Virginia. The ribs, brisket, turkey, and pork sausage were all from local farms and cooked over a wood fire on a massive stone barbecue pit out back. You could get your meat selection wet or dry-rubbed, and it always came with a homemade hot-dill pickle.

Temperance people and teetotalers who wouldn't set foot in any other bar would still go to The Rose for BBQ carryout and a gallon of sweet tea. The rest of the Rose's clientele would come for lunch or dinner, soft jazz, and the best BBQ in the state.

Over the years, the Rose changed hands half a dozen times and was even sold out of the family for a spell. During Prohibition, The Rose became a private club but was still in the business of serving spirits, all be it to people who knew the password, Swordfish, and could get past the

bouncer at the door. Then, twenty years ago, Nathan Rose MacLearnan, a direct descendant of Mary's, bought the bar and brought it back under family control. The most recent ownership change didn't produce many apparent modifications. The decor was pretty much the same, and the mouse problem was still an undeniable topic of conversation; "Get a cat!" people would tell Nathan weekly. However, once a MacLearnan family member was back in control, The Rose once again was offering the best small-batch whiskey in West Virginia.

Nathan was silent about where he got the whiskey and would never show anyone the bottles it came in. However, if you were on the list, you could order a shot of the best shine everyone said they had ever tasted. For ten years, that whiskey was the talk of the town. And then, ten years ago, it disappeared. All Nathan would sadly say is that his source for the whiskey had gone away.

Twelve years ago, The Rose got some "competition" when Dolion's Place opened up directly across the street from The Rose.

Dolion's Place was run by the son of the only mortician in Busby. Nobody could believe that the Undertaker would invest in a bar, knowing how tight with a buck he was. Therefore, where Dolion got the money to open a bar was a mystery and the cause of much speculation, as was where he got the moonshine he sold.

Where The Rose had history, Dolion's Place was an upstart. Where The Rose was comfortable and had good food and drinks at reasonable prices, Dolion's had expensive, watered-down liquor and overpriced food that wasn't up to the standards of your average high school cafeteria. What Dolion's Place did have was loud, abrasive rock music, red and black velvet covering most of the walls, an abundance of chrome, and scantily clad women servers. Dolion's Place had a reputation that many an illicit deal could be made in the dark booths that circled the bar's interior.

Dolion's Place was why the previous mayor, the honorable Jesse Wainwright, tried to regulate both bars in town. Mayor Wainwright was an unapologetic, strong-willed Baptist and considered all intoxicating drink the devil's work; furthermore, you didn't even want to get him started on the unwholesome atmosphere at Dolion's. Busby was a decent family town, gosh darn it, and he would make sure it stayed that way.

Exactly one month after Wainwright was sworn in as mayor, the two bars found their hours of operation curtailed. More ordinances followed, including a Modesty Provision passed by the City Council and signed by the mayor. No more could servers in any Busby establishment comport themselves with immodest dress.

The mayor's plan failed spectacularly.

The Rose had no problem working within the constraints of the new laws. Dolion's Place, however, suffered greatly and had no intentions of following the new rules.

No sooner had the business hours and dress code gone into effect for both bars than public drunkenness in the town and vandalism complaints went through the roof. As soon as Dolion's had to close, its customers would buy beer, drive to the town square, and get raucously drunk right in front of the Busby courthouse. By morning, each of the town's four jail cells was filled. By noon, those people were bailed out, and the process would repeat itself.

Every morning, the gazebo in the town square was littered with empty beer cans and bottles. The smell of people using the park's trees as convenient urinals made business owners demand a change. Soon after that, and without fanfare or public announcement, the two bars were allowed to resume their prior hours of operation.

The general public thought both bars were a release valve of sorts for the rowdier aspects of the citizenry. Therefore, their continued operation was accepted. What the people didn't realize was that the mayhem was all due to Dolion paying certain people to instigate and cause trouble.

Other proposals were put forth by the mayor to improve the town; however, the town council, with freshly greased palms courtesy of Dolion, wouldn't bring any of them to a vote. As a result, the Honorable Mayor Wainwright never finished his term. Instead, he resigned from his office and headed out of town to parts unknown to do missionary work, never realizing to what degree he had been manipulated.

Soon after that, Dolion was elected Mayor. That was eight years ago, and his first official act was to fire the standing police chief and bring in Jarred as his police chief and enforcer. His second act was trying to run The Rose out of business.

Right on time, Porter came walking down the sidewalk and onto the porch. He took a moment to look at each of the cats and raised an eyebrow at seeing a Person with them. Then, finally, he sat down and stared at Joel with quiet regard. After first meeting his gaze, Joel bowed his head and stared at the porch floor.

"Ah ken sees it's ye Ghost, it guid ta see ye. How ye daein?" Porter softly woofed.

Joel continued to stare at the floor and did not respond. Finally, after a minute, Joel softly meowed an apology. "I'm sorry, Porter. It's ma fault that Obadiah wus killed. I shoulda been wit him, lettin' em know there wus danger. After seeing him shot, I was a coward, an' I ran."

"Awe, ye aff yer heid," the dog responded. "Did ye pull the trigger? Naw! Obadiah en gone to the mine withinot ye lots o' times. If ye had ben there, ye would ben deid to."

"I coulda warned him he was being followed. He didna' hafta die," the old grey cat wept, tears running down his whiskers.

"Ach, yer daft. Obadiah ken ye he bein followed. That's why he came back to the cabin, ta get his gun," Porter replied.

"Obadiah came back to…to the cabin?" Joel looked up, confused, staring at Porter and then into the assembled faces staring at him.

"What happened that day, Porter?" Belle asked the old Highland Collie.

For a man of his years, Oba was in excellent shape. Even so, he knew that sooner or later, the trip up and down the mountain would become insurmountable. This thought was in the front of his mind while he was making the second trip of the day to the mine, and he noted that he felt fatigued.

Oba didn't try to carry the grain, propane, and other materials he used at the mine anymore. Instead, these days he used a mule named Daisy to ferry all the supplies to the still and the cabin. The neighbor who loaned him the mule got a bottle of shine, and Daisy got a bowl full of carrots and apples, so it was a good arrangement.

If the family business had a future, Oba knew he would eventually have to bring someone in and teach them about distilling. The thought that he might be the last Maclearnan to make whiskey bothered him more than he liked to admit.

"I wonder if Marie would wanna carry on the tradition?" he said aloud to the mountain on his trek. "I'll ask her when she gits' home from school,"

About halfway to the mine, even without Ghost and fatigued, Obadiah knew he was being followed. His sixth sense, what he liked to call his hillbilly sense, told him he wasn't alone.

Right after Ghost had run off to have fun, Oba was approached by one of the Bouncers from Dolion's Place, asking if he could buy a couple of pints of shine for the upcoming holiday. Oba knew this young man as a former star football player for the local high school team. The young man would probably have gone to college and turned pro if he hadn't damaged his knee in his senior year. Since graduating and turning twenty-one, he had been a bouncer for Dolion.

Oba was sorry that such a nice kid had to work for Dolion, but he knew the young man's family needed the money. "Sure, Paul," Oba said to him. "I'll go git' the whiskey an' meet you outside your work." Then, as an afterthought, he said, "I'm sorry you have'ta work for a louse like Dolion."

"It's all good. Thanks," Paul said and walked away. He had no idea why his boss had asked him to buy the whiskey from Obadiah, but he was paying him to do it and told him he could keep the whiskey. Getting a couple of free pints of Oba's whiskey was a win in his book.

Oba returned to the cabin and looked around to see if Ghost was back, but to no avail. He was probably having fun somewhere and wouldn't be home for hours. *No problem,* Oba thought. *I will just run to the mine, grab the whiskey real quick, and make this last delivery.* So, for the second time today, he was going up to the Mine. But this time, halfway there, he knew he was being followed. Oba would stop every so often and appear to catch his breath, but in reality, he was listening to the sounds of the mountain and what they were telling him.

A bird being startled—leaves rustling—twigs breaking, told him that somebody was behind him. He paused again and took a surreptitious glance down the mountain. Sure enough, it was Dolion, and that fool Jarred, trying to hide behind a couple of trees. The two of them sounded like a pair of wild boars tromping through the forest.

You're an idiot, Dolion, Oba thought, but then also chastised himself. *I shoulda brought my gun right off,* Oba admitted.

Well, I know what to do, Oba thought to himself. *Instead of heading to the mine, I'll loop around an git' back to the cabin. I'll grab my shotgun and set up a surprise for these two morons.* He quickened his pace and got far enough ahead so they could not immediately see him. Then, he made a sharp turn and headed back down the mountain toward home. After a few minutes, he could see the cabin up ahead with a bit of smoke curling out of the chimney.

Porter's head came up when the door opened suddenly, and his owner hurried in. Obadiah quickly crossed the room and grabbed the gun that was propped against the wall. Checking that a shell was in the chamber and that the safety was on, he quickly went back out the door.

Porter got up, stretched, and moved toward the door to see if Oba would reappear. The pup noticed the door wasn't completely shut when he got close. By using his paw and scratching at the jamb, he opened the door just enough to squeeze through. Then, trotting out onto the porch, the pup saw his owner hurrying back into the woods. Curious, Porter decided to follow, to see what was going on.

Dolion was furious that they had lost sight of Obadiah. The simple plan of catching and roughing him up had disintegrated into chaos. Looking down at himself, he was also annoyed that brambles were stuck on his pants and mud on his shoes.

"I'm going to have to dry clean all these clothes," Dolion muttered in disgust.

"What'd ya say, boss?" Jarred asked.

"Nothing. Never mind. Do you see Oba anywhere?" His enforcer shook his head.

If Dolion had any confidence in Jarred at all, he'd let him handle this alone. But, sadly, he was forced to be here himself. Stopping to catch his breath, he took out a monogrammed handkerchief and wiped his brow.

"He must have seen us following. Damn!" Dolion said, turning to his assistant. "I am going to head back to the trail. I want you to loop around the other way and call out if you see him. We will meet back at the cabin and wait for him there. It doesn't matter anymore to be quiet," he told his fixer.

Porter ran through the wood, following his owner's scent. Up ahead, a slight rise gave a good look at the trail that would either take you back to town or up the mountain. Coming to a stop, the Highlander Collie saw Oba, his gun pointed at the ground, arguing loudly with another man. Taking in the scene with his excellent eyesight, he spotted Ghost as he came into view on the other side of the path. Porter was about to run to his owner when he saw a third man approaching Oba slowly from behind, something in his hand.

Before Porter could bark a warning, the third man raised his hand, and two shots rang out. His owner pitched forward and fell to the ground, unmoving. Suddenly, Ghost let off such a terrible howl of anger and despair that the heavens themselves must have heard. This caused the gunman to bring the pistol around and fire several rounds at the cat. The bullets made a wet, thumping noise as they hit the ground around Ghost. The grey cat let off one more howl and then disappeared back into the woods.

The old Highland Collie stopped his story and shook his head. Belle had tears in her eyes, and Joel hung his head, shaking slightly. Then, after a minute, Giblet got up and walked over to his friend and began licking his head, letting him know it would be okay.

Mittens had been translating Porter's story for Anne. Although she spoke cat fluently, understanding other animals was not part of her gift.

Addressing Joel, Anne said: "You see, Joel. There was nothing you could have done. Obadiah knew he was being followed without you. Chances are, had you been there, you would be dead also.

"I shouldna run away. I shoulda stayed an' fought."

"No. That's just guilt talking," the old Protector informed him. "You are a smart and capable cat Joel, but you have never been trained like I was trained and like I'm training Belle."

"Listen to them, Joel. You helped me with the guilt of my brother's passing. You pointed out that there was nothing I could have done. It took a while for your words to sink in, but you were right. So, give yourself the same consideration," Giblet added.

"Ghost, whits fur ye'll no go past ye," Porter added.

"What?" Belle asked the Collie.

"It's a highlander sayin'. It means whatever is meant to happen to ye will happen. So, stap feelin sorry fer yerself or I'm going ta skelp yer wee behind," Porter added with an emphatic woof.

Everyone was quiet for a while. All were listening to the night sounds when the only human present decided to speak.

"Let's review what we have; a murder that is ten years old, no physical evidence, in a town controlled by a police chief and mayor, both involved in the murder, and our only witnesses are a cat and dog," she nodded at Porter and Joel.

"We have no murder weapon, body, or forensics, and if we talk to anyone in town about this, the perpetrators will get wind of our investigation. If we are lucky, they will simply write us off as crazy and ignore us. If we are unlucky, I might get committed to an asylum, and all of you will end up in the pound. Of course, the worst-case scenario has all of us ending up like Obadiah."

"Yup. That about sums it up," Belle admitted in a more cheerful voice than the situation deserved.

"We're doomed," Giblet added.

Everyone was quiet again when Porter decided to add.

"I ken whaur's Obadiah is buried, and whaur's the gun is," the Highlander offered.

CHAPTER VIII

Clues Missed

"Be careful and watch your back," Marie warned,
grabbing her backpack and turning to leave.

12:00 Noon,
First Cat Lunch

Professor Russell Macgregor was bent over the table in the little library's study room, quietly scanning genealogy records of the town of Busby. In the early years, the town was little more than a trading post, nestled in a quaint little valley. It was a place to pick up supplies and rest your horses. Then, in the early nineteen hundreds, coal was discovered, and a short-lived coal-boom happened. Coal company money financed several civic projects, including a rail spur, court house, police station, and public library. The holdings, particularly its genealogical resources, were impressive for such a modest library.

Most of these records were from old church rolls. Lists of births and deaths went back to the town's founding by the trapper Abraham Busby almost two hundred years prior. It seems the town owed its location to an amusing collection of circumstances; a broken wagon wheel, a couple of tired horses, and Abraham's desire for a drink of whiskey.

Abraham Busby was a back-woodsman, trapper, and carpenter who was perpetually bored. Ever since he left the family farmstead in

Massachusetts, he was always looking for new challenges and scenery. However, Abraham had one skill that went with him wherever he went which gave him the greatest pleasure; he enjoyed learning how to make wine, beer, and spirits. This passion traveled with him wherever he went.

He made wine on the family farm with the grapes his parents grew. After he left, he learned how to make Applejack while passing through Connecticut with their bountiful apple orchards. Later, he learned how to brew beer with some German immigrants in New York and spent time working for them. However, his stop in western Pennsylvania, where he was schooled in the art of distilling whiskey, made Abraham happiest. He spent a year in the area, gathering knowledge about the grains, fermentation, and distillation of American whiskey. When it was time to move on, he took this distilling knowledge and a full whiskey barrel with him.

Abraham's original destination had been Tennessee, but his wagon broke down in a quiet and picturesque valley halfway across West Virginia. Climbing down from the wagon and muttering a few choice expletives, he surveyed the damaged wheel. *Tarnation, that wheel will have to be rebuilt before we can go on,* he thought.

The first thing the town's founder did was unhitch his horses and lead them over to a small stream for a drink. Then, being thirsty himself, he tasted the water and was amazed at the quality; there was just a hint of sweetness, and the dissolved minerals gave the water a wholesome taste. *A little of this added to my whiskey would taste good,* he thought to himself.

The second thing the Founder did was tap the small whiskey barrel in the back of his wagon. Abraham sat and thought about fixing the broken wheel for a long time but never quite got around to it. According to legend, Abraham built two things that first summer; a crude homestead and a still, assembled from components he had brought from Pennsylvania. Busby moonshiners like to point out that Abraham built the still first.

TOWN OF BUSBY.
POP. 3

As suspected, the water in the valley helped produce some of the best whiskey Abraham had ever tasted. When his homestead was more or less complete, the town of Busby was born. It had a population of three—one human and two horses.

It seemed Busby was a natural stopping point for people heading to the southwest from the east. Early on, it was other backwoodsmen that wandered into the valley, had a drink, and a few decided to stay.

The early pioneers used the new town to sell furs they trapped and as a comfortable place to winter in. They could rest their horses and pick up provisions, especially whiskey. Then, a few families decided to call the valley home, and pretty soon, there was a small community. In the early years, the population stayed small, under a couple of thousand people.

The discovery of coal in the 1890s brought much-needed infrastructure, railroads, and better schools. Coal money also brought more families to Busby, each looking for a fresh start. One curious statistic attributed to the coal boom was increased whiskey production. Anyone acquainted with mining can tell you that coal miners are a thirsty lot.

Gradually, coal became less accessible, and after World War I, the last of the mines closed, and the companies moved on. Busby became just another of the numerous communities hidden away in Appalachia's mountains and valleys. Then, as Prohibition was made law in the 1920s, Busby's second (unofficial) industry took off, whiskey production and bootlegging.

Law enforcement looked the other way in exchange for a cut, and multiple families became distillers with the help of gangster money flowing in from the big cities. Fights broke out among a few of the families as they vied for market share. The Whiskey Wars of the 1920s were fast and bloody. The victor would take over the operation of the vanquished until they themselves became a target because they had one still too many to protect.

Russell was reading about a particular bloody moonshine feud in 1925 when a voice called from behind him; "When you concentrate, you really concentrate." Marie MacLearnan observed him from the doorway. "How about you call your wife, and we all go to lunch?"

Sitting up and stretching, Russell replied, motioning to the paper he was reading, "This is great material for my research, really interesting." Seeing the clock, he was surprised that he had been sitting for over three hours. "Yeah, lunch sounds great. What place do you have in mind?"

"It's a tavern a couple of streets over called The Rose. Best food in town," she replied confidently. "When you call your wife, ask her to meet us there. It's straight down 2nd street from the college."

Marie returned to the library counter. Grabbing her small backpack and walking to the front door, she was just turning the sign on the Library door to "Closed For Lunch" when Russell came up.

"Shirley is going to meet us there," he announced.

"Great. What were you looking at before so intently?"

"Birth and marriage records. I'm trying to get a feel for the town and the people whose families were in the whiskey trade," Russell replied. "Making whiskey before 1862 was generally not a problem. But, when they passed the Revenue Act of 1862, a lot of whiskey production went underground because the makers didn't want to be taxed. But, of course, that was fifty-eight years before Prohibition and all the problems that law created."

Russell continued, "Some of the old death records list 'distiller' as their occupation. I'm curious if the descendants of these families continued the tradition of making their own spirits."

"You know, my uncle Obadiah was a whiskey maker," Marie related. "He had a secreted still somewhere on his property. Our family, according to legend, has made whiskey since we came to this valley, years before the Civil War.

"Really? Did you ever find it?"

"No. But I understand people have been looking for it for years."

"Was the whiskey good?" Russell asked.

"I tasted it many times at family functions, and as I recall, it was delicious. People used to swear that his whiskey was the best in the state," Marie said with pride. "He never told me where the still was or anything about distilling. That knowledge disappeared with him."

"I'm sorry he isn't around. I bet he would have been a great person to interview. Was your family involved in the Whiskey Wars?"

Marie shook her head. "I don't think so. The family was more interested in making small batches of excellent whiskey, not big batches of lousy product." As they walked up the street, Russell observed that many of the families in town were related in some fashion.

"Absolutely," Marie agreed. "There are so many large families that married off daughters and sons that most of the older families can claim at least one relationship with each other. In fact, The Rose, where we are going for lunch, is owned by a relative on my mother's side of the family, the Roses."

They turned the corner and started up 2nd street toward The Rose. Up ahead, they saw Shirley approaching from the opposite direction. They arrived at the entrance to The Rose at the same moment. The outside looked quaint and nondescript. The building was covered with red brick, with two big windows on either side of the French-style doors. There was a glass transom across both doors and an old-fashioned, well-worn brass door handle on each door. A simple sign over the door read— The Rose.

Contrasting with The Rose's homey look and feel was Dolion's Place across the street. Its façade was covered with shiny metal and blackened glass. And in case anyone forgot who owns the establishment, Dolion's name was emblazoned in bright red neon over what looked like a black-metal, studded door. A huge bouncer with a perpetual frown completed the unsavory, unwelcoming visual.

"Wow," Shirley observed, looking over at the other bar. "I'm kind of glad we're not eating there."

"Yeah, that's the mayor's place," Marie confirmed. "Flashy trash. But you didn't hear that from me."

They entered the Rose and were immediately greeted by Nathan, the owner who stood behind the bar. The room was more or less square, with ten-foot ceilings covered with hammered tin panels. An old-fashioned belt-driven set of ceiling fans placed strategically around the room moved the air efficiently and completed the retro 1920s look of the place.

Miles Davis was softly coming out of stereo speakers in the corners of the room. It looked like all the tables were taken with people enjoying their lunch.

Nathan waved at Marie and pointed to three open barstools at the end of the bar.

"Do you mind sitting at the bar?" Marie asked her guests.

Shirley and Russell smiled and shook their heads. When all three were seated, Nathan greeted them, "Hi Marie. What can I get you and your friends to drink?"

Before answering, Marie turned to her guests and asked, "Do you trust me?"

Both smiled and said sure.

"Nathan bring us three plates of the barbeque special of the day, dry-rubbed with sauce on the side, three hot pickles, and three sweet teas," Marie ordered.

"You will not be sorry," she said to the Macgregors, opening a napkin and placing it on her lap.

Nathan put in the order and returned to his customers. "You're the guy writing the book about moonshine?" he observed while pouring their tea from a glass pitcher.

"Wow, does everybody in Busby know we're here?" Shirley grinned.

"Small town," Nathan said. "Fresh faces stand out around here," Marie added.

"In answer to your question," Russell began, "It's more of a history of distilling and unlicensed whiskey-making since 1900. It seems from my research that for many small moonshine operations, making whiskey was more of a family tradition and a demonstration of skill, rather than a racket or money-making scheme." He paused to savor a sip of tea.

"My thesis is that there was not that much money in the running of your own still until Prohibition was in effect. And after prohibition ended and the big manufacturers got back into the business, the income for home distillers dropped off again. So, why distill your own whiskey if not for continuing a family tradition?" Russel wondered.

"Perhaps the artistic satisfaction of producing a real quality spirit," Nathan responded. "I look forward to reading your book when it's done."

It was then that the food arrived. The three plates were piled high with ribs, smoked brisket, and smoked turkey. On the side was a bowl of savory, private recipe BBQ sauce, and a large homemade hot pickle. Conversation ceased as the trio began eating. Not long into the meal, Marie and Russell both exclaimed how good the BBQ tasted, even the hot-pickle, which neither one had ever had. Hot pickles were not generally something you could find very easily in Connecticut.

Nobody could finish all their food so they requested three to-go boxes. After a busser took the plates away, they made small talk about the classes Shirley was teaching. Eventually, Nathan came over with their to-go boxes and a silver tray with three shot glasses filled with a deep amber liquid.

"Here, taste this," Nathan said as he set a shot glass reverently in front of each of them.

Russell picked up the shot glass and smelled it appreciatively. It was definitely whiskey, with a woodsy scent and a faint sweetness in the undertone. Sipping the whiskey carefully, he noted the many layers, with the lightest being vanilla and oak. Other flavors he couldn't immediately identify, but all critical to the experience added to the body of the spirit.

The finish wasn't hot or bitter but rather lingered on the pallet, the whiskey flavors continuing to evolve. It was by far the best whiskey Russell had ever had.

"Wow, this is really good," Shirley commented.

"I don't think I have had a finer whiskey," Russell admitted, holding the half-full shot glass up to the light.

"This really tastes familiar," Marie observed, smiling at Nathan.

"It should. It's your uncle's special batch recipe," Nathan said with a smile. "This is the purest example of the art of distilling. Although Obadiah never charged what he could have gotten for his whiskey, he was happy that people enjoyed it."

"Did you add any water to it?" Marie asked

"I did indeed," Nathan confirmed. Then, reaching under the bar, he produced an antique glass bottle with crystal clear water inside and an eyedropper in the top.

"This is pure spring water from up on the mountain. No chlorine or other additives. I only add a few drops to unlock and release the bouquet and the multiple layers in the distillation. You never add ice to this whiskey; it would ruin it. The British think we are heathens when we add ice to our spirits,"

Looking at Marie, he said, "I only have about half a bottle left. I just wanted your guests to taste the best example of the whiskey maker's skill."

"You know, Dolion has been after me since Uncle Obadiah went missing. He keeps offering me lots of money for this recipe," Marie said, saluting Nathan with the shot glass. "He seems to think I know where it is."

"I hope you never sell it to him," Nathan responded. "That man would ruin the legacy with his greed and shortcuts."

"No problem there. I have no idea where the recipe is," Marie admitted before finishing the last few drops of whiskey.

"Thank you for this," Russell said, saluting with the empty shot glass. "This was an extraordinary treat.

You say that Obadiah never charged what he could have gotten for his whiskey?" Nathan answered with a nod. "Then this right here reaffirms my thesis," he said with a smile. "Distilling because of tradition and as a demonstration of skill."

"I'm sorry, but I have to get back for my afternoon class; if you could bring the check, we will settle up," Shirley said, finishing her shot. "I wish we could stay here the rest of the afternoon and chat!"

"This is my treat," Nathan told his guests. "Bring the family in sometime, and you all can have dinner here."

Marie, Shirley, and Russell thanked Nathan again and promised they would return. Before leaving the bar, Marie pulled Nathan aside and asked, "Is Dolion still giving you trouble?"

"Yeah, he still wants me to sell to him," Nathan admitted, frowning slightly. "But as long as more than half the town eats here and Judge Fraser is a regular, he has to tread carefully."

"Be careful and watch your back," Marie warned, grabbing her backpack and turning to leave.

While the parents were at work, Anne and Mittens planned to check out the scene where Obadiah had been buried. Porter assured them that he knew exactly where the grave was and that it wasn't very far away.

"We can't very well take the kids along for a body hunt," Anne thought out loud.

"I'm not so sure," Mittens replied. "Perhaps if you tell them we are just going for a hike in the woods. You certainly don't have to tell them the reason."

"Not bad. Not a bad idea at all," Anne admitted. "I can just say we are going out for some exercise."

Thinking for a moment, she added, "When the parents come home, I'll tell them we're going to explore the mountain tomorrow. Can you make sure Porter understands to meet us, so he can lead us to the grave?"

"I'll see him in a little while and get all the details settled," Mitten purred. "I'm pretty sure Giblet won't want to go; he can stay here with Iko."

"What about Joel?"

"I think he'll be coming with us. After last night, he's blaming himself less and wants justice," Mittens said confidently.

Just then, a small black blur came tearing through the kitchen, followed by two giggling children.

"Slow down, you roughnecks," Grandma Gaumont called out to the Children's retreating backs.

"We're playing with Belle," they called out, disappearing into the hallway.

Belle was having fun distracting the People-Kittens while Mittens and Anne talked. She ran down the hallway and turned toward the base of the steps. Racing to the top, she waited for the People-Kittens to catch up. Soon both were running up the stairs toward her, giggling non-stop.

Belle had an idea. As soon as the People-Kittens caught up, she took off running down the hallway and into the bedroom where Giblet was taking his early afternoon nap. The little black cat leaped into the air and landed on the bed directly in front of her best friend.

"Whaa, what's going on?" the tabby-cat exclaimed with a start, having been rudely awakened from a sound sleep.

Belle grinned with an evil smile. Then, timing her next move to the arrival of her pursuers, Belle jumped over Giblet and off the other side of the bed, heading back for the door. Both People-Kittens followed her path onto the bed, over the scarcely awake tabby, and off the other side of the bed.

"I'm going to get you for this!" Belle heard Giblet howl as she ran down the hallway and back down the steps, both People-Kittens in hot pursuit. At the bottom of the steps, she made a turn for the kitchen with Cassidy following and Christopher right behind.

Getting to the bottom, Christopher grabbed the top of the banister newel cap to help him make the turn. Suddenly, the whole top came off in his hand, and he tumbled forward, crashing onto the floor.

Mittens and Anne heard the crash from the kitchen. Sharing an I-told-you-so look, they ran to investigate. They found Christopher on the floor, startled and holding the top of the newel cap in his hand but otherwise appearing unharmed.

"I'm sorry. We're just playing. I didn't mean to hurt the steps," Chris said, pleading his case to Grandma Gaumont.

Mittens was annoyed with her protégé and glared at Belle for the mishap while Anne asked everyone, "Are you okay?"

"I'm okay. But I broke Mommy and Daddy's steps," Chris said, chagrined, holding the cap out to Grandma.

Anne took the cap and looked at it and the newel post. "You didn't break it. The top just popped off. Your Dad or I can put it right back together with some glue," she consoled the Child. "But, I think your game is over, don't you?" she asked both Children, including the sheepish black cat, with a glance.

Two yeses and one meow followed as Anne led them back to the kitchen for some lemonade.

Mittens and Belle looked at the newel post without the top. "This isn't our house. You have to be more careful, so the Man-Person and Women-Person don't have to repair any damage," the old Protector reprimanded her apprentice.

"Okay, you got it," Belle assured her.

"Come on. We have a plan for tomorrow, and I want to fill you in," Mittens informed Belle as both cats walked back to the kitchen.

The newel post was original, hand-built, and installed over a century before when the house was still under construction. The newel post was a simple rectangular pine box painted white and adorned with decorative trim rather than a solid piece of mahogany or oak like you might find in a more well-to-do home. The cap was made from a flat pine block, with a small hand-carved pineapple screwed to the top. Pineapples were long the symbol of friendship and hospitality and were often included somewhere in houses of the era.

Giblet watched the episode from the top of the steps. He saw where the top was off the stair post and how it appeared to be hollow. Then, being as curious as the next cat, he wondered what was in the opening. However, his curiosity was not more potent than his lassitude. There was still napping to be done, so he gave a deep sigh and trotted off back to bed.

If Giblet, Belle, or anyone looked into the newel post, they would have been surprised. At the very bottom of the post was a roll of yellowed papers carefully wrapped in a scrap of old oilskin cloth and bound by a strip of leather. The documents were over a hundred years old and written by candlelight with a quill pen. Anyone reading them would see it contained the recipe for the MacLearnan whiskey, courtesy of Mary Rose MacLearnan, along with her frank appraisal of some other distillers in the area.

It seemed that Mary Rose considered herself the self-appointed spirits critic of Busby. Names and reviews of a dozen other families' whiskey were listed on the document. All in all, it was a humorous and frequently biting critique.

A few additional notes were added at the very bottom of the papers. Around 1900, someone decided to write down the exact location of an abandoned mine on the MacLearnan property. Finally, another author documented a few tweaks to the whiskey recipe in modern ink fifty years ago. After that, the papers were hidden and lay undisturbed inside the post where Obadiah had hidden them.

CHAPTER IX

The Journey

Finally, without the distraction of driving, the young
woman looked at their furry passenger and said,
"Welcome to New York."

Cat Time:
Ten Years Earlier—Pennsylvania.

Ghost had lost track of how long he had been on the road. He knew it
had been well over a human-week and that he was still heading north;
the sun coming up on his right was proof enough of that. Still, he didn't
know exactly where he was.

At night he would find someplace as protected as possible against the
cold, rain, or snow, if there was any. His thick Russian Blue coat kept
him warm enough, and his paws were toughened by the outdoor life he
had led with Obadiah.

As soon as he thought of Oba's name, the image of him lying on the
ground, not moving, came rushing back. That bleak image kept him
going. As long as he was heading somewhere, it kept his mind off recent
events. When exhaustion finally overtook him, he slept, but then the
dreams of what happened came back. He'd wake up from the coils of the
nightmare and keep moving, trying to outrun his torment.

So far, his ability to obtain food had kept him from starving. An open trash can was a good food source, or a good-hearted Person's handout also provided nourishment. Only a couple of times had he needed to hunt game for his dinner. Fortunately, Ghost was a backwoods cat, born and bred to hunt.

A couple of days ago, Ghost had been cutting through several backyards when a voice called out, "Hi there. Where are you going in such a hurry?" an older woman with kind eyes had asked him.

Ghost stopped and scrutinized the older woman in a light-blue coat. However, when she slowly approached him, he backed up, and she got the message.

"You aren't very trusting, are you?" she asked rhetorically, in a soft voice. "I can't blame you; perhaps it's because we haven't been introduced. I'm Sue."

Ghost watched her movements, not moving toward her but not running away.

"Wait here," she said and disappeared back into her house. Then, a moment later, she returned with some cat food on a plate and a small bowl of milk. She set them down in the yard and backed away.

Ghost approached the food and sniffed it. It smelled like the kind of tuna Oba sometimes got for him. Then, drooling, he began eating, all the while keeping a watchful eye on his benefactor.

To her credit, Sue didn't approach the hungry grey cat. Instead, knowing that an animal needs to make the first move, she sat on the back doorsteps and patiently watched him eat. After a few minutes, Sue looked at the darkening skies and spoke to her guest once again.

"I've got an idea. Stay here, and I will be right back," she said and disappeared again into her house.

A few minutes later, she was back with a box that had a fluffy towel in it. She placed the box on the porch and placed a different bowl, this time filled with kibble, in front of the improvised cat bed.

"You can sleep in this tonight if you want to," she said gently. "The porch roof will keep you dry, and tomorrow, we can figure out our next step."

"Rrrowll," Sue heard from her guest in between bites of food. *Thank ya, ma'am–* was what Ghost said in cat with his West Virginia accent.

Ghost finished the tuna and sat down to begin grooming, debating his next move.

"You're not from around here, are you?" he heard. Turning, he spotted a red fox watching him from the tree line.

"No," he replied, giving his full attention to the fox, out of respect, not fear.

"Where are you from?" the fox asked.

"Busby, West Virginia," Ghost said with a sigh.

"Going to or running from?" was the next insightful question.

"I guess you could say I'm runnin' from." Then after a pause, "Frankly, it's a tangle." Then, changing the subject, Ghost asked the fox, "Where the heck am I?"

"Northern Pennsylvania, about half a day's walk from the New York border," the fox offered. "You have come quite a-ways."

"I was lucky. I hitched a ride on a lumber truck."

"Where are you headed?" the fox asked conversationally.

"I don't know," Ghost replied. "North, I reckon."

"Well, it's pretty dark out right now. You might as well stay. The woman has put a bed out for you," the fox observed. "This Person has always been nice to the local animals. If you stick around, she might adopt you."

Ghost looked at the box on the porch, and the bowl of kibble put out for him. Then, deciding there was nothing to gain by heading out in the dark, he walked to the box and began making-biscuits with his paws. After a minute, he settled down and looked at the night.

"Good night," he heard the fox call as he moved with a lissome grace back into the woods.

"Good night," Ghost said quietly to himself.

The hike into the woods began in the morning after the Man-Person and Woman-Person had left for work but before the heat of the day had set in. Anne's preparation for the day started right after breakfast. First, she ensured she and the Children wore long pants and long-sleeved shirts to minimize exposure to ticks and poison ivy. Comfortable shoes were a must; to this end, Anne had a broken-in pair of hiking boots, and the Children had waterproof trail boots that their parents had bought for the trip.

The shirt Anne picked was comfortable, but what was really important was that it covered the conceal/carry holster she wore on her hip. Inside that holster was her Model 36, Smith & Wesson Chief's Special. During her time on the Torrington police force, Anne always carried a Beretta 92FS, 9mm semi-automatic pistol. However, her backup gun (BUG) was always her Chief's Special, a present from her late husband, and very dependable; revolvers, you see, didn't jam.

In addition, she brought a fiberglass tactical hiking stick to top it off her ensemble. The hiking stick was a gift from her late husband, who bought it mainly as a joke. It was made from carbon fiber that was both lighter and stronger than wood or aluminum and was adjustable in length. The handle had a piece of soft rope that went around the wrist so you wouldn't drop it by accident, and it had a compass built into the end cap. If you unscrewed the top, you would discover a hollow, waterproof cavity that concealed, among other things, all-weather matches, a small knife, and a survival saw. Topping it all off, the hiking stick came with a slim rescue whistle that produced over 100 decibels of sound. The manufacturer claimed the whistle could be heard over a mile away if you blew hard enough.

When Mr. Gaumont presented the walking stick to his wife, she laughed and asked how much danger he thought she got into on the well-worn paths of Torrington? Today, Anne was glad to have the walking stick along.

Before leaving the bedroom, Anne checked her revolver to ensure five 38 special caliber rounds were in the cylinder. Then, snapping it shut, she glanced down at Mittens and said softly, "Better safe than sorry." The old Protector nodded in agreement, then jumped off the bed and went downstairs.

Ten Years Before...

Ghost awoke with the dawn, unsure where he was. He had been dreaming of the cabin and Oba and it took a moment to realize how much his life had changed. Sitting there, he decided he wouldn't stay with this woman, even though the temptation to do so was great. He needed to get further away from his failure.

After finishing all the kibble and water, he headed out. Since it was cloudy that morning, Ghost couldn't get a fix on the sun for his course, so he decided to follow alongside a road he thought was going in the right direction. Gazing at a road signpost, he saw US 206 / Pennsylvania Ave. Not knowing where it led didn't bother Ghost until he saw a bridge up ahead.

Cars were traveling over the bridge at a brisk pace. There wasn't a sidewalk, but there did seem to be enough room along the edge to walk across the span. Ghost was about halfway across when a pair of hands grabbed him around the middle and lifted him in the air. Utterly unprepared to be picked up, he acted instinctively with a sharp hiss and a swat with his front paws.

"Ouch! That stung. You dumb cat." Ghost turned his head to see a bearded young man had grabbed him. "I'm just trying to make sure you aren't run over," the young man continued.

"Hurry up. We're holding up traffic," another voice called out from a car that was stopped on the bridge.

"Roll down the back window!" the young man called to the driver. "And be ready to put the window up quick."

Ghost was carried to an open car window and unceremoniously shoved through. As soon as he landed on the back seat, the window went back up. The young man who grabbed him ran around the car, pausing a second to wave an acknowledgment at the stopped vehicles behind them, and quickly got into the passenger's seat. His sister, who was behind the wheel, put the car into drive and they continued across the bridge.

"Did he get you?" the young woman asked while concentrating on traffic.

"Yeah, but it's not much," the young man confirmed. "I think I startled him."

"Where do you want to take him?" she asked.

"We'll take him home with us for the moment until I decide what to do with him."

"See if he has a collar," the young woman suggested.

"I'll take a look. I didn't see one when I grabbed him, but I was in a hurry."

The young man turned and looked at the grey cat in their back seat. Ghost, for his part, sat quietly and returned his gaze.

"I don't see any collar, but he looks kind of dirty. I think maybe he's a stray," the young man suggested.

"What's he doing back there?" the driver questioned, not wanting to take her eyes off the road but also not wanting the car torn up by some wild cat.

"Nothing. He is just sitting there, watching us," he reported.

After about thirty minutes of driving, they pulled into a driveway of a small house. "Go get Mom and the pet carrier," the young woman suggested. "I will stay here with our guest."

The young man quickly got out of the car, just in case the grey cat tried to follow him out the door. However, Ghost continued to sit patiently and stare at his would-be rescuer. Finally, without the distraction of driving, the young woman looked at their furry passenger and said, "Welcome to New York."

Anne, the two People-Kittens, and three cats left the house in Busby to begin their hike in the woods. As Mittens had guessed, Giblet wanted to stay behind, saying a hike in the woods didn't sound fun at all. Iko said she did want to come along on the hike but couldn't get Anne to take her with them.

Up the street from the house, Porter the Highland Collie joined them. "Hi, Porter," Belle called out cheerfully. "How are you?"

"A'm daein fine," he said with his thick accent. "Whit aboot yersel?"

"Everyone is ready," Mittens answered. "Lead on."

Porter took point with Mittens, followed by Belle and Joel; Anne and the two Children covered the rear. Soon, the town was left behind, and they began their trek up the mountain trail.

Belle was under strict orders to keep Joel in sight at all times, but it didn't seem like the old grey cat intended to run. For his part, Joel kept quiet, lost in his own thoughts. He stared at the trail and the scenery as if trying to connect to the life he had here once.

"Do you recognize this area, Joel?" Belle asked her friend, but the old grey cat stayed silent.

It was a beautiful day for a hike, and soon, everyone but Joel was enjoying the picturesque landscape. Thirty cat minutes into the hike, Porter indicated that Oba's old cabin was up ahead. "Okay," Mittens responded to the dog. "Let's go there first; I want to check it out."

Mittens turned and meowed to Anne that she wanted to see the cabin, and Anne nodded. A few minutes later, the cabin came into view.

What had once been a comfortable, well-maintained little mountain cabin was now a wreck. Most of the split-rail fence was down and the area was overgrown. The cats and People could see that all the windows were broken and there wasn't a front door anymore. The roof was missing a few wood shakes, and trash was strewn around.

Anne looked the cabin over but did not want to venture onto the porch, which looked dilapidated and unsafe. She also wanted to keep the children from trying to enter the building.

"Please, can we go in?" both kids pleaded. "No, it's not ours, and it does not look safe," came Anne's firm response.

Mittens looked at the porch and calculated that it could hold her weight. She climbed the stairs and looked in the open door. She saw that there wasn't any furniture left, and the floor was strewn with beer cans and other trash. Mittens noted aloud that the old rock fireplace looked like it had been used recently.

"'Em People-Pups from ta toon. They use this place ta hang out and drink beer," Porter reported as he joined her. "After ta polis couldna' find Oba, Marie got tha place. She took all the furniture and Oba's stuff to her hoose."

Joel joined them on the porch with Belle by his side. He didn't say anything; he just looked bleakly at the ruin of the cabin. More than anything, Joel wanted to remember the good times in this cabin. However, the destruction he surveyed denied him that comfort.

"Do you think there are any clues here that will help us?" Belle asked softly to all who were assembled.

"Ah widnae' think," Porter responded. "When Marie en ah came back ta move Oba's things out, tha cabin looked ramshackled li'ah it wus' searched. Ah didnae' ken if they found anythin.'"

"I will bet my whiskers that it was Dolion that searched the place. I wonder what he was looking for?" Belle questioned out loud.

"He was lookin' fer a way to Obadiah's still," Joel said. "It's all he ever wanted."

Ten Years Before...

The mother came out to the car with a pet carrier and a pair of heavy leather gloves while the young woman got out of the front seat and waited for instructions.

"Open the cat carrier and put it on the back seat," the mom said. "I will go around and push the cat into it."

The young driver opened the rear door and set the carrier in the car with the door open. To everyone's astonishment, the grey cat walked calmly into the carrier on his own accord and laid down. The mom reached in and closed the door.

"That certainly is a well-trained cat," the sister observed. "I really wonder if he's a stray?"

"Yeah. I didn't expect that," the mom admitted. Then turning to her son, she said, "Let's take a look at that hand."

"It's nothing, just a scratch. I think he was startled when I picked him up," the son reported.

"Well, it probably is nothing, but he broke the skin with his claws. You realize he will have to go to the pound," the mom said, examining the hand. "Go inside and wash it and put some antiseptic on it."

"Do you have to take him to the pound? Couldn't we watch him here?" the sister pleaded.

"No. We have to let the professionals do their job," the mom said, taking Ghost to her car. "I'm sure he will be fine."

The mom drove to the animal shelter with mixed feelings. She didn't think the cat was sick or dangerous, but she could not take the chance with her son's health. She arrived, walked in with Ghost, and placed the carrier on the front counter.

A young woman attendant with a gamine face and several piercings looked up and asked, "Can I help you?

"Yes," the mom replied. "My son rescued this stray and got scratched accidentally. Can you check to see if he is registered and if he has been vaccinated? He hasn't acted sick or dangerous at all."

"Sure, no problem." She put on her own pair of gloves and opened the carrier door, but before she could pull Ghost out, he walked out calmly and sat on the counter. "That's unusual," the attendant observed before passing the chip-wand several times over the grey cat.

For his part, Joel looked at the attendant and noted her purple hair. *You certainly didn't see purple hair in Busby,* he thought. "Yankees," he meowed.

"No microchip that I can detect," she announced. "We'll have to quarantine him for ten days to ensure he doesn't have rabies."

"Then what will you do?" the mom asked, already knowing the answer.

"Well, he isn't that young. We'll give him a chance at adoption if he doesn't display aggressive behavior. But if he isn't adopted, he'll be put to sleep," the attendant said sadly. "We never have enough room for all the animals that need homes."

The mom was upset but knew the attendant was telling the truth. There was always more need than resources. "Why don't People spay and neuter more?" she said out loud.

Then, making a decision, she said, "I will be back in ten days." She wrote down her name and phone number and handed it to the attendant. "Don't do anything with him without contacting me." She gave Ghost one more long look and left the shelter.

The attendant took Ghost into the back and put him in a cage with food and water. "Sorry, buddy," the young woman said as she left.

Ghost looked around at several other cats and a couple of dogs in different cages. Then, before closing his eyes, he muttered to himself, *It figures.*

Porter and the cats jumped off the porch and rejoined Anne and the People-Kittens. Mittens meowed at Anne and informed her that there didn't seem to be any valuable evidence left in the cabin.

"Okay, let's move on to our next stop," she told the senior Protector.

Porter once again took the lead, and the group moved off. Finally, they reached the place on the trail where Oba was shot. He turned around a woofed, *we're here,* to Mittens.

Joel looked at the area and had no trouble remembering what had happened on this spot ten years ago.

"Ta killen happen here," the dog indicated a spot on the trail. "Oba was aboot here, Dolion aboot thar, an' Jarred wus hidden in tha bushes," the dog woofed, pointing with his nose.

When Porter was finished, Mittens translated all of it for Anne.

Glancing at the kids who were up ahead on the trail and picking her words very carefully, she asked, "Where is Oba now?" Anne knew that Children tended to be little tape recorders and constantly repeated things they heard at the worst possible moment, so she couldn't very well ask about the location of a body.

Porter once again moved off with everyone following but didn't have to go very far. The group stopped at the base of an old oak tree. There wasn't anything to indicate a grave except perhaps that the ground had a small, somewhat sunken appearance.

"Aye, Oba be aboot thar," Porter confirmed.

Nobody approached the unmarked grave, and Anne glanced around, happy to see that the kids were ignoring them. She quickly took out her cell phone and snapped a few pictures of the area, then used another app to mark the exact GPS coordinates.

"Oba's shotgun is buried whit em," Porter informed them.

"Thank you for showing us this, Porter," Mittens told the Highland Collie. "Did they bury the murder weapon with Oba, also?"

"Naw, Jarred didnae widnae part wit that gun."

Do you know where he keeps it?" Belle asked.

"Aye, it hing on his hip just yesterday," the Collie confirmed, to the general astonishment of Belle and Mittens.

"You mean he still carries the gun?" asked Belle, still trying to get into the swing of the Highlander's accent.

After being filled in on the conversation, Anne replied, "He carries the murder weapon around with him? Good lord. The man's an idiot."

"That's Jarred," Joel confirmed

Taking in the surroundings, Anne addressed Mittens and Belle, "A metal detector should be able to detect the shotgun easy enough, and I have marked the coordinates. I think it's time we head back. We have accomplished what we needed to do today."

"Hold on there a minute," Joel asked the group before they departed.

Walking carefully to the spot where Oba lay, he stopped and bowed his head. Anne guessed what he was doing and took the kids up the trail, so he could have privacy. The animals, however, gathered around the grave and bowed their heads in respect to both Oba and Joel.

After a minute, Joel straightened up and turned away from the grave. Then, looking Mittens straight in the eye, he said, "Let's git' these murderers."

CHAPTER X

Reconnaissance

Joel watched the pliers with dread and thought about what would happen next. *"If he does what I think he's going to do, I'm going to be sick."*

Cat Time:
First Breakfast

"Grandma Gaumont talks to Mittens," Cassidy piped up while eating her cereal and watching a children's program on PBS.

Anne kept stirring her tea but turned toward the table where the family was having breakfast. Likewise, Mittens stopped eating her kibble and turned toward the Child.

"We all talk to the cats, honey," the Woman-Person told her daughter while the Man-Person smiled. "We also talk to Iko."

"No," she said quickly. "She talks to them like you talk to Daddy."

"That's nice," the Man-Person said as both parents returned to their tablets, reading the morning news.

"And the cats talk back," Cassidy continued between mouthfuls of oatmeal.

Anne walked to the kitchen table with her tea, sat down, and smiled at the Child. Christopher, she was glad to see, ignored everyone while he watched the kid's show and had his cereal.

The Man-Person decided to play along with his daughter's game and asked, "What do Grandma and the cats talk about?"

"Oh, all kinds of stuff. Yesterday, they talked about where a body was buried," Cassidy explained and returned to watching her program.

At that statement, both parents looked at Anne with questioning eyes. Back at the cat bowls, Giblet started coughing, like he swallowed wrong, and Belle said in a sotto voce, "Uh oh."

"Oh, we were telling ghost stories on our hike in the woods yesterday," Anne said easily. "We saw an abandoned cabin in the woods that looked spooky, but I wouldn't let the kids get close."

"She gets her imagination from your side," the Man-Person said good-naturedly to his wife. "Telling her Shakespeare plays like *Macbeth* at bedtime? I mean, really. You're the English major. Couldn't you pick something fun like *The Tempest?*"

"What about the bedtime stories you tell about the Jacobite rebellion and the battle of Culloden?" the Woman-Person retorted with a smile. "The cost for child therapy runs about a hundred dollars an hour."

"At least she will be the smartest kid in the third grade," Anne suggested, and both parents laughed.

After breakfast, both parents gathered their things, kissed both Children goodbye, admonished them to *"be good"* with a smile, and left for work.

After they had gone, Anne cleaned up the kitchen table and spoke casually to the Child finishing her meal.

"Cass, do you understand what the cats say when they talk to us?" Anne asked as nonchalantly as she could while rinsing the bowls in the sink.

"Oh sure," the little girl responded. "They're fun to listen to. Mittens is the smart one, and Belle is young like me. Oh, oh, and Giblet is the grumpy one."

"Nailed it," Belle whispered into Giblet's ear.

"Go ahead and joke," Giblet responded softly. "This could become a big problem."

"Do you understand what Iko says?"

"No. She's a dog," Cassidy replied, lacing her words with reproach as if an adult should already know this.

Anne and Mittens shared a look but remained silent. As soon as Cassidy had finished her cereal, Anne told her and Christopher to go upstairs and get dressed. They all would be going to the store in a little while for groceries.

As soon as they were sure they were alone, the important conversation began.

"This is going to get a little more complicated," Mittens meowed.

"We will have to keep in mind who is around when we talk, that's for sure," Anne agreed. "Fortunately, Cassidy has a vivid imagination," she pointed out, motioning to the kid's program still playing on the TV with anthropomorphic animals in human clothes.

Mittens nodded and turned to leave. "Belle and I are going to do some investigating today. Then, after the People-Kittens are in bed, we'll gather and go over everything tonight."

"Where are you going?" Anne asked.

"I am absolutely certain you don't want to know," was Mittens' amused answer.

All four cats and Iko gathered in the bedroom after Anne and the Children had left for the store. Mittens stressed the importance of being discreet when Cassidy was around. Belle was proud of the child's abilities, but Giblet, as usual, looked worried.

"How much trouble will it cause if the People-Kitten hears us and repeats it," Giblet asked the group.

"She is the youngest and, as I said, has a rich imagination," Mittens observed. So, I don't think the parents will be too concerned with what they believe to be inventive stories. Still, we must be cautious."

"She may have a great imagination," Giblet meowed, gathering every cat's attention. "But, haven't you noticed that Cassidy is *very smart* for a People-Kitten? She figures things out extremely fast. Furthermore, haven't you noticed her reading stuff on her Mom Person's computer? She is reading all the time, and it is much more advanced than the People-Kitten show she was watching downstairs," he informed them.

"What's your point?" Belle asked.

"I'm not sure I have a point other than to suggest that People-Kitten is special in many ways that could become a problem for us," Giblet summed up.

"Does the boy People-Kitten understand us?" Joel asked, taking an interest in the conversation.

"No, I don't think so," Mittens replied.

"I thought you said that it wasn't common for people to have the ability to understand cats?" Joel asked Mittens in a follow-up question.

"It isn't supposed to be. Until I met Anne, I had never encountered anyone who could understand us. But, now we have two people at opposite ends of the age spectrum, who live next door to each other, that can understand cat."

"That's a coincidence, isn't it?" Giblet remarked.

"Weird," Belle observed, and Giblet nodded.

"I don't believe in coincidence," Mittens said. "We will revisit this topic. But right now, we need to stay focused. We need to check out Dolion and gather intelligence.

There are two places I want to look. First, Dolion's house is right up the street. Second, I want to have a look at his business. Porter told us that he owns a bar in town and a funeral home. We need to take a look at each of these places and report back what we find," Mittens outlined. "Belle, I want you and Giblet to check out Dolion's house, but be careful; look out for Lucinda."

"You all be careful, young missy," Joel piped up. "That Lucinda is sneaky an' evil."

"You don't have to go, Giblet, if you don't want to," Belle meowed at her best friend. "I can handle it."

"Absolutely not. You need someone to watch your tail," Giblet insisted, although he looked worried. "I'm coming with you."

"Good," Mittens said to the pair. "Keep in mind what Joel just told you. Watch out for Lucinda, and if confronted, run away—don't engage. Do you understand?" Mittens ordered.

Both Belle and Giblet nodded, understanding the seriousness of the matter. Then, turning to Joel, she asked, "Do you know where Dolion's bar and other business are?"

"Unless they moved em, I surely do. An' I knowa way there that we won't be seen."

"Good," she said to Joel. "You two," she said, addressing Belle and Giblet one more time, "**Be careful!** We will meet back here this afternoon before the People get home from work."

"I want to go to," Iko said to the group. "I want to help."

"Iko, I am serious when I say we would love to have you along. But a good-sized dog walking around will attract too much attention during the day. We need to be unobserved for as long as possible so Dolion and Lucinda don't know we are investigating them. I promise you are a part of this team."

Mittens locked eyes with Belle, and she nodded. Both of them guessed Dolion, Lucinda, and even Jared would eventually catch wind that their past was being looked into, and then all kinds of heck would be unleashed. They would try to get as much done as possible before that happened.

Iko woofed that she understood why she couldn't come along, but she seemed let down.

Giblet and Belle nodded at each other and started for the door, but before they got there, Joel spoke up one more time; "I'm not foolin' around. That there Lucinda cat is bad as they come," he announced. "Don't ya turn your tail on her an don't believe anythin' she says."

"Don't worry, Joel," Belle said cheerfully. I will keep an eye out for her."

After both cats disappeared from the room, Mittens turned to Joel, "Lucinda, has you that troubled?"

"She's a killer," he said simply. "An' I worry."

"Welcome to my world," Mittens confessed as they headed for the door.

With a reluctant Giblet in tow, Belle cut through several backyards to the house where Dolion lived. The first thing both cats did was walk around the whole property in reconnaissance. It looked like most of the other residences on the street but with a couple of striking exceptions.

The backyard was totally enclosed by an eight-foot-high wooden privacy fence. Until now, every privacy fence Belle had ever seen was only six feet tall. This enclosure looked much more uninviting. The single entry through the fence had no handle on the outside, meaning you could only open the gate from inside the yard. In Belle's opinion, the NO TRESPASSING sign on the gate was superfluous.

"Somebody likes their privacy," Belle observed, and Giblet nodded.

The other exception was the front door of the house. Where everyone else on the street had a storm or screen door on the front of their homes, Dolion had a wrought-iron security gate with two cameras and motion sensor flood lights covering the area. Both cats went up to the gate to examine it closely. They could tell it was made from heavy-gauge, black iron with two deadbolts securing it. It was decorative but also very functional.

"See those hinges?" Belle said, pointing with her paw. "Those are ball-bearing, heavy-duty hinges. That gate weighs a ton, and I bet it could stop a car from ramming through it."

Looking closely at the gate, Giblet agreed, "Somebody certainly feels the need for security. We'll never get in through here," he observed. "Let's see if there is any way in, around back."

Both cats slowly walked along the tall privacy fence, looking for any weakness.

Belle put her paw on the pine boards that made up the fence and extended her claws. "With my claws, I could get up and over the fence, but you probably couldn't follow me," Belle observed.

"You are not going over that fence alone," Giblet intoned. "That's final."

"Worrywart," she teased but agreed not to try it.

They saw something had dug under the fence line as they approached the farthest corner of the yard. There was a gap, too small for a person to get under but large enough for a smaller animal like a cat. Whoever had dug this breach had done so behind a bush so it couldn't be seen from the alleyway.

"It looks like an animal comes in and out here," Belle suggested.

Sniffing, Giblet said, "I smell a cat and at least one other animal."

"Here goes nothing," Belle said and dove under the fence before Giblet could object.

Giblet looked at the space under the fence and swore a cat oath at his friend for taking chances. "Belle, are you okay? What do you see?"

From the other side, she called back, "Come here, Giblet. You've got to see this!"

Joel and Mittens were sitting in a different alley behind the funeral home Dolion had inherited from his father, deciding what to do. So far, the duo had made excellent time with their mission. Joel had set a brisk pace that got them first to the restaurant, then to the funeral home. Despite his age, Joel was acting like a cat half as old.

The stakeout at the restaurant proved one thing, Dolion was still very active in the moonshine business and was getting whiskey from many different sources. While the two cats watched, several vehicles arrived to make deliveries.

The delivery routine was always the same; a car would pull up, and the driver or a passenger would get out and knock a pattern on the back door; three knocks, a pause, and two more knocks. Only then would the back door open, and a pair of sweaty and stained kitchen workers come out, collect the whiskey and carry it back into the bar. The engine would be kept running during the delivery, which usually lasted less than a couple of minutes.

"That there is Williamson," Joel had pointed out as he saw different People make deliveries. "He and Obadiah used to trade a bottle every now and then."

A rusted-out truck came up, and one of the men got out; he looked like they hadn't bathed or cut their hair in the last decade.

"Them is the Boscal Brothers," Joel narrated. "Their shine is only good fer killing insects or as a cure for sight."

"Well, it looks like Dolion controls most of the moonshine business for this area," Mittens commented.

"Yup. Taken over Oba's still would've got him a monopoly, fer' sure," Joel admitted.

"Well, we are going to make sure his greed results in his downfall," Mittens promised. "Let's go see the funeral home and then head back. But first, I am going to look in the kitchen window for a second."

Mittens ran over and climbed onto the windowsill. She gazed into the kitchen window for a moment, then sprang down to rejoin Joel.

"If I didn't know better, I'd swear you wus' turnin' green," Joel observed. "Whatcha see?"

"Enough to know that this place should be quarantined as a biohazard. Come on, I need some fresh air."

Giblet was struggling to get his girth under the fence. Belle had gone back under the fence because she correctly guessed it would be more helpful if she could push Giblet from the rear. Finally, with a supreme effort, Giblet squeezed through the opening and into Dolion's backyard. What greeted him there astounded him.

There was such an agglomeration of decorations and yard ornaments that it assaulted the eyes. To call the backyard gaudy would have been a compliment.

"I think we need to add to the list of crimes Dolion should be charged with," Giblet said to Belle as she came up to his side.

"Yes," she agreed. "Dolion has murdered good taste."

Both cats made their way to the back door and noted a pet door.

"Do you think Lucinda is inside, or is she with Dolion?"

"I don't know," Giblet admitted. "You're going to go inside the house anyway, aren't you?"

"It would be a shame to waste the trip," Belle admitted.

"Fine. But if you hear any People in there, you come right back out. I guess I don't need to tell you to be careful." It was a testament to Belle's accomplishments as a Protector that Giblet figured she could handle herself. "I will stand watch here unless you call me. If you're not out in ten cat minutes, I'm coming after you. If I howl, you get out immediately."

"You got it," Belle promised and disappeared into the home.

The décor inside the house was not an improvement. Unfortunately, the Great Cat in the Sky had passed over Dolion when she gave out good taste, Belle thought.

She walked through the kitchen into the hallway and closed her eyes. Then, not moving a whisker, she listened with all her cat senses, just like Mittens had taught her. She heard nothing and felt no other presence. Satisfied that she was alone in the house, she began her quick and thorough search of the home. She swiftly identified several bedrooms, a couple of baths, and the living and dining rooms. One of the bedrooms had a desk and not a People's bed. *This must be his office,* Belle thought.

There were no books in the office, just a desk, computer, and more disgusting décor. Looking at the dark computer screen, Belle sighed and thought to herself, *I really need to learn how to use one of these things.*

She jumped onto the desk and began looking over the papers that were left out. Belle knew from experience that People kept their money in places called banks. For instance, her People had their accounts at a bank in Torrington. However, after examining Dolion's papers, he appeared to have at least five bank accounts. One account was in the Busby Savings and Loan, but three others were in banks in the Cayman Islands, and one was in a place called Panama. Judging from the amounts in each account, the good mayor of Busby was doing very well for himself.

Belle jumped off the desk and made one more pass around the room. No safe that she could see. A locked drawer in the desk intrigued her, but she didn't have anything that could pick a lock, so it would remain a mystery. *A raccoon on the team would also be a big help,* she thought.

On her way back to the pet door, Belle passed the living room with its black-velvet wallpaper and zebra-striped furniture. Belle made a gagging motion as if to cough up a hairball and quickly turned her head from the visual assault.

Satisfied with the scouting foray, she went back through the pet door and into the yard. "Did you achieve what we came here for?" Giblet asked softly.

"Yeah. I think I found some interesting information about the mayor, besides his horrible taste in décor," she confirmed. "Let's go."

As they headed for the gap under the fence, Belle stopped and motioned to one of the dozen statues around the yard. "What does this one remind you of?" she asked Giblet.

He thought for a cat minute and promptly said, "Greek revival meets Gaudi meets Ludwig The Mad."

She laughed at his description as both cats made a hasty exit. Once they were safely back in the alley, Belle listened again, hearing nothing; she was confident they had finished their mission unobserved.

No sooner had the pair gone out of sight than a large white Persian cat emerged from behind some trash cans where she was hidden. The cans' residual odor had masked her scent nicely. Furthermore, the Persian knew how to cloak her presence by making only natural sounds you would hear in nature.

She recognized those two cats from the previous night. Swearing a few cat oaths to herself, Lucinda decided she needed a plan to deal with this new threat.

Joel and Mittens arrived at their last stop, Dubghall Memorial Funeral Home—run by the Dubghall family for the previous one hundred years. It was an older, stand-alone building, traditional and quaint. Apparently, Dolion either hadn't had a chance to tawdry up the place or had the sense to know Busby residents wouldn't like their loved ones going to a funeral home that looked like it belonged on the Vegas strip.

"At least there's no neon lights and bouncers," was Mittens' comment that caused Joel to smile.

They walked around the funeral parlor, completing a perimeter check. There were entrances on either side of the building where guests could come and go. Apparently, it was early, and no visitations were going on because both sets of doors were locked up tight. In the rear of the funeral home was a garage where they kept the hearse. They found the garage door open and an employee detailing the long, black vehicle and listening to loud rock music. "When he's distracted, we should be able to get inside," Mittens meowed to Joel. "He'll never hear us over the noise."

Joel and Mittens watched and waited for a few cat minutes. Then, when the worker bent over and stuck his head inside the hearse to vacuum the floor, they darted into the funeral home.

Mittens stood for a minute, her eyes closed, listening. She heard the worker outside and perhaps one or two more in the building, but they were not close. Then, confident that she and Joel could avoid them, they began their search.

"What are we looking for?" Joel whispered to Mittens.

"I'm not sure, just keep your ears up and look around. Let me know if you see anything suspicious."

Both cats crept slowly around the various empty parlors. As they had suspected, no visitations were going on, and the parlors were empty. The door to the office was closed, with the muffled voices of two people within. This annoyed Mittens because she really wanted to search in there. However, the door to the basement was ajar. Nodding at one another, both cats slowly descended the stairs into the non-public areas of the funeral home.

"I'm not anxious to see dead People," Joel admitted.

"We will take a run-through and have a quick look. Then we're out'ta here," Mittens reassured her companion.

Both cats went into what must have been the embalming room. Two surgical-looking steel tables with drains in the middle were in the center of the room, empty of occupants; Joel was grateful to see. Taking stock of the room, Mittens noted shelves with various jars of chemicals along one wall, and on the other wall was a long sink with foot pedals that controlled the water. A stainless-steel wheeled table with various surgical instruments sat between the two tables. All in all, it reminded her of what she read about operating rooms.

Without warning, Mittens heard the footfalls of two People and something else coming down the hall. Looking around frantically, she hissed to Joel, "Follow me." Both cats slid under the shelves and pressed themselves against the back wall.

Two workers in black suits pushed a casket through the swinging doors and into the room. Despite the suits, the men had a rough, callous air about them. *The suits are like lipstick on pigs,* Mittens thought. Sensing their dimwitted nature, she named them Mutt and Jeff.

Mittens slithered to the edge of the shelf so she could watch the two men. Mutt opened up the casket and started removing things from the occupant. A ring, watch, and cufflinks were all taken and dropped into a bag Jeff was holding. As soon as they were done collecting the jewelry, Mutt went to the rolling steel table and retrieved a pair of surgical pliers.

Joel had joined Mittens at the edge of the shelves, and both cats watched transfixed. Seeing the pliers, both cats dreaded what would happen next. *"If he does what I think he's gonna do, I'm gonna be sick."* Joel thought.

Jeff opened the deceased mouth as Mutt reached in with the pliers and tugged back and forth. A moment later, he pulled out the pliers and grasped in its jaws was a gold tooth.

They opened the bag once again and dropped the tooth in. "Put this in the Dolion's lockbox," Mutt said. "He'll be over to empty it later." Jeff grunted, "Uh-huh," and left the room.

Mutt dropped the pliers on the table, then closed and locked the casket. Mittens watched as he wheeled it back out of the room.

"Wow," was all Mittens could bring herself to say.

"Yeah, I'm gonna be sick. This," Joel said, waving his paw at what they had just seen, "This is exactly the kind of man, Dolion is."

Nodding in agreement, Mittens said, "Let's go," and she led the way back out of the room and out of the funeral home.

Cat Time:
10 Years Before–Upstate New York

The ten days were up tomorrow, Ghost thought. *I guess they realize now that I don't have rabies.*

Except for being fed and watered daily, the staff had left Ghost alone. The only visitor who spent time with him was the vet tech, who checked him for rabies symptoms. After each check, she would smile and tell him to *"keep up the good work."*

"Your ten days are up tomorrow, aren't they?" a dog woofed at him from across the room. "Will your owner come and get you?"

"I don't have no owner...anymore," was Ghost's reply.

"Well, don't lose hope," added a cat in the cage below his.

"Yeah, okay," came Ghost's reply before putting his head down. *"I wonder what will happen tomorrow,"* wondered Ghost as he closed his eyes.

CHAPTER XI

Straw Men And Paper Tigers

"Byde yer time, an follae Jarred," Porter suggested.
"He will leid ye to tha lowie."

Cat Time: Six hours after Cat Dinner

In what was fast becoming their meeting time, all the cats, Iko, Porter, and Anne, gathered on the front porch after the family went to bed.

Mittens brought the meeting to order, "Belle, what did you and Giblet find out?"

"Dolion has absolutely no taste!" Belle said almost immediately, to the general amusement of those gathered.

"He has zebra-striped furniture, velvet-textured wallpaper, and a gold People toilet," she disclosed.

"That figures," Mittens admitted. "But bad taste isn't against the law. Did you find anything we can use?"

"I saw papers on his desk for people bank accounts in someplace called Grand Cayman and Panama. I counted at least four different off-shore bank names and saw the amounts. There is a lot of People money there. Unfortunately, there was a computer and a locked desk drawer I couldn't get into," she added.

"Neither of us knows anything about People computers," Giblet added.

"Did ya run into Lucinda?" Joel asked, concerned.

"No, but she will know we've been there. We had to crawl under the fence to get in, and undoubtedly we left our scent," both cats admitted.

"Joel, do you think Dolion can communicate with Lucinda the way we can?" Anne asked. "Do you think he will know these two were in his house?" she asked, motioning to Belle and Giblet.

"I don't think he can talk to cats tha way you do if that's what ya'r asken'," Joel responded. "Hear tell he got Lucinda because she wus an expensive cat, an' Dolion likes to have expensive stuff."

"Did you see any cameras?" Mittens asked.

"No cameras inside the house that I could see," Belle confirmed. "Unless they were very well hidden."

"There are cameras covering the front door and an eight-foot-high privacy fence around the backyard," Giblet reported.

"Okay, good reconnaissance," Mittens replied. "I think Joel and I found at least two sources for Dolion's illegal wealth," she told the group.

"When we wus at his bar, we seen several whiskey deliveries goin' in the back door," Joel informed them. "It looks like he controls all bootlegging in the valley an' beyond."

As an afterthought, Mittens contributed, "I looked in the kitchen window and never eat there for the sake of your health."

"I ken tell ye tha' skellum Dolion hae approached Marie mair times for Oba's whiskey recipe," Porter told the group. "Hae really wants that."

"Did she ever give it to him?" Belle asked.

"Ye're aff yer heid," Porter responded immediately. "Marie hate's that bastart."

"The most interesting discovery we made was at the funeral parlor," Mittens announced. "We know where he is getting some of his money, besides bootlegging, I mean."

Everyone stared at Mittens with rapt attention. Then after a dramatic pause, she revealed, "Dolion is a grave robber!"

While the two Protectors and their friends were meeting on their front porch, Jarred was in his office at the police station, finishing up his latest entry in his journal. In reality, it was a computer file, meant as an insurance policy for the day Dolion turned on him. Every illegal act he witnessed or was involved in was recorded in graphic detail, including date, time, and location. He kept the information on two thumb drives. One was always on his keychain, and the other file was hidden at his home as a backup.

When Dolion was elected mayor, he had made Jarred Hebeto police chief, even though he had never had a day of police training in his life. Jared's only knowledge about being a cop was gleaned from kitschy 80s and 90s cop shows on television. But, to Dolion, the lack of training didn't matter. Furthermore, the fact that the three career deputies in the Busby Sherriff's office despised the chief and had no respect for him didn't matter either.

Slavish, unwavering loyalty was the only thing Dolion valued, and so far, Jarred was loyal. However, the loyalty only traveled in one direction, to Dolion and him alone. As slow on the uptake as he was, Jarred guessed correctly that he would need something big if his boss decided to turn on him. That was when he started the file.

To date, the diary was more than a hundred pages, including a few photographs that he'd managed to take over the years. Shakedowns, payoffs, bank accounts, and the occasional violent crime were recorded in graphic and misspelled detail. That the same information could be used against himself didn't bother Jarred. In his mind, he thought he could work a deal to deliver Dolion in exchange for a free pass.

There was a knock on the door, and one of the deputies stuck their head in. "I'm outta here, boss. Good night."

"Night," Chief Hebeto responded and returned to his two-finger typing.

"You saw him robbing graves?" Anne exclaimed with shock.

Mittens and Joel exchanged looks, and Joel said, "You tell 'em. It made me sick."

"We snuck downstairs at the funeral home and saw two of Dolion's people strip the body of all the valuables. Then one opened the deceased's mouth while the other pulled out a gold tooth," Mittens concluded, to the general nausea of the team.

"Oh, my cat," Belle said, shaking her head.

"They would need to send the jewelry well outside of town to move it; if they sold it around here there is too much chance someone would recognize it," Anne speculated. "And, it's anyone's guess where they are processing the gold taken from the bodies."

"It looks like Dolion is running quite an extensive criminal organization," Giblet offered. "The restaurant, the bootleggers, and grave robbing; the number of People working for him is much more than I expected."

"An' aw tha lowie from be'un mayor," Porter reminded everyone.

Everyone stopped and stared at Porter, trying to translate what he had just said. "Ach, ye sassenach's. Ah' dinnae ken how ye don't get Scots," he said with exasperation.

"Wha' Porter said wus he's also gettin' paid fer his job as mayor," Joel said, helping out.

"I don't understand. How does Dolion get away with all of this?" Belle asked the group. So many people must know what a wicked man he is, and still he was elected mayor?"

"I tell ya, young missy," Joel began. "Dolion is nothin' but a paper tiger. His power over this town is because of his charm, an' outwardly he keeps his hands clean. He gits others ta do his dirty work. He is a very smooth grifter, but ultimately he is a coward. They work fer him because he makes 'em money, an' the good People don't stand up to him because he is a bully."

"Aye, an' Marie wus here when he wan. I heard her sayin that reprobate made promises he didnae keeps and straw-men arguments agin his opponents. Inna, he changes the subject if questioned too strongly," Porter informed the group.

"Obadiah had him figured out a long time ago. He jus' didn't think he would sink to murder," Joel concluded.

"Do you think we can find out where they keep the stolen property?" Anne asked Mittens. "Finding stolen property in Dolion's possession would go a long way to securing an indictment."

"We couldna followed them two without be-in seen," Joel said. "We wus lucky to git outta there as it was."

"Joel's right," Mittens agreed, deep in thought. "Dolion probably goes to great lengths to hide the stolen property. And his accomplices are probably just smart enough to see two cats following them and wonder why."

Everyone was quiet for a time, thinking.

"Byde yer time, an follae Jarred," Porter suggested. "He will leid ye to tha' lowie."

Cat Time:
Ten Years Before–Upstate New York

"You don't want to stay here with us, do you, Joel Grey?" the Mom-Person asked, looking at him.

The name had no meaning for him for a few seconds, then Ghost remembered this new family had renamed him, Joel Grey. He turned away from the window and looked at his benefactor. They stared at each other for a moment, and then he turned back to stare out the window once again.

Ghost had been with the family for a little over a month after being rescued from the pound. The day he got cleared for rabies, the mom had turned up just like she said she would. He had to admit, that surprised him. When he was removed from the quarantine cage, the other animals barked and meowed congratulations.

During his time at the pound, he had seen several cats and dogs go into a room, and none of them returned. Ghost figured it was just a matter of time until that happened to him. He had resigned himself to that fate because there were always more dogs and cats than there were good homes. More People needed to read the posters on the walls of the pound about spaying and neutering their pets.

After inoculations against rabies and several other viruses, he was neutered and sent home with the Mom-Person. On second thought, Ghost meowed loudly that he could have done without the neutering part. But, he understood the reason.

Throughout his month with this new family, Ghost had been treated very well. He had an impossibly small box to sleep in, kibble and freshwater were always provided, and he had the run of the house.

But he was not a happy cat.

His thoughts continued to dwell on Obadiah and the reason for his leaving. Hearing the shots ring out and seeing him fall and lay unmoving in the woods haunted his dreams. So, Ghost did not sit on the new People's laps; he did not purr. Instead, he sat in the window every day and looked at the pasture behind the house.

"You want to continue your journey," the Mom-Person added sadly. She wished she could understand why the new cat wasn't happy.

The son and daughter came into the room to see their mother watching Joel Grey. She named him after the famous song and dance entertainer she had admired for decades.

"He's still not happy, is he?" the son asked.

"No, I can't get him to meow, purr, or sit on my lap," the mom conceded.

"We're both packed," the daughter announced, getting around to why they were there. Then, motioning to her brother, she said, "He's going to drop me at my school on the way back to his college."

"That's good. Drive safe, and both of you call me when you get back to your dorms," the Mom instructed. "I have to run up to Torrington next week to meet with my dissertation adviser."

"What are you going to do with Joel?" the son asked.

"I'm taking him with me because I don't want to have to board him so soon after leaving the pound. And, the Macgregors said they already have a cat, so I should bring him with me."

"That's a good idea," the daughter agreed.

CHAPTER XII

The Unexpected Trip

"Oh, poop," she thought…

Cat Time:
Five hours before Cat Breakfast

After the meeting broke up, Porter went home, Anne went to bed, and the cats found places to curl up. As usual, Giblet laid down in the master bedroom, and Belle curled up next to him. However, her mind wouldn't settle. She was concentrating on the problem of Dolion and how to bring him to justice.

They knew where the body was, who committed the murder, and where the murder weapon was. But how could they tell People without Anne sounding crazy or the killers getting away? So, while Giblet snored, she tried to devise a plan.

There has to be an answer; it feels close, Belle thought. Even so, fatigue soon won, and Belle closed her eyes. It seemed like only a few minutes when suddenly she was jolted awake. The phenomenon was back, and multicolored glitter was swirling around in the air in front of her. This time, however, she stuck out her paw and began tapping on Giblet's head and whispering out the side of her mouth, "Wake up! Wake Up!"

Giblet stirred slowly and mumbled, "Wa...what? Is it breakfast already?" Then, opening his eyes fully, he saw the vortex and was quickly fully awake.

The face of MacKayla appeared, and once again, Belle heard the voice in her head, *"Belle, you have to be there for Joel. His guilt will..."* the rest of the warning faded out, like a radio that loses the signal.

"MacKayla? What...Is that you?" Giblet meowed, his eyes locked on the floating ethereal face.

"I am protecting Joel," said Belle. "We know about Obadiah and who is responsible. We are going to bring him to justice!" she pleaded. "I don't know what you want me to do?"

However, just as before, the energy MacKayla used to keep the doorway open was fading fast. Then, before it closed completely, Belle thought she heard *"...the cat."* And then the room was once again dark and quiet. The People in the bed had slept through the whole thing.

She turned to her friend and softly meowed, "Did you see it?"

Trembling, Giblet nodded weakly. Then, he reached out with his paw to pat Belle, but the shaking only got worse.

"Let's go find Mittens and tell her. This can't wait till morning," Belle advised.

The two friends went to Mittens and shared the events they had just witnessed. She listened quietly to the whole story and was as disturbed as they were about its implications.

"I swear it was MacKayla," Giblet informed Mittens. "The only difference was that she looked a lot younger."

Mittens nodded at the information. "Keep this quiet, the two of you," Mittens instructed. "We don't need to worry Anne. She doesn't need to add spectral aberrations to everything else she has to deal with."

"What about Joel?" Belle asked.

"I think we should keep this between us," Giblet offered. "No telling what he would do with this warning. He might get his hackles up and head out and confront Dolion. That would be a mistake."

"Agreed, we keep it to ourselves for the time being and keep our eyes open and whiskers fluffed," Mittens instructed.

"However," she continued, "one of us should stay with Joel all the time. From now on."

Giblet and Belle nodded and returned to the master bedroom; however, sleep for both of them was elusive. Furthermore, Belle was worried about the implications of the second visitation. Were they on the right track in their efforts to protect Joel? Why did Mackayla appear before her for a second time? Why not appear before Mittens or Giblet? There had to be a reason.

She wasn't convinced that MacKayla's visits should be kept from Joel any longer. But, at least Giblet saw the aberration this time, so she wasn't worried that she had imagined it.

Belle didn't want to go against Mittens and Giblet's orders to keep the visitations to themselves, but MacKayla had approached *her* twice, and that had to mean something. Making her decision on how she would handle it, Belle finally closed her eyes, tucked her nose into her paw, and went to sleep.

The following day, the cats met Anne to plan their strategy while Iko kept the Children busy in the backyard. Once again, they decided to split their forces. Giblet and Belle would try to follow Jarred, while Mittens and Joel would reconnoiter Obadiah's old mine and see what, if anything, was left.

Anne had an outing planned today with the kids and couldn't help. However, she planned to do research into Dolion and Jarred surreptitiously when she returned.

"The local paper has its back issues online. So I will start there and then widen my research to surrounding communities," Anne explained. "I wish I could go with you to see the mine."

"It's probably better if you are not seen with us," Giblet suggested to Anne. "Best to stay here and not arouse suspicion."

"Then it's settled. We meet back here before the People come home from work," Mittens summarized. "Stay safe. And, don't take chances," she instructed Giblet and Belle...but mostly Belle.

"Don't worry, Mittens, Giblet is with me," Belle said with a smile.

"Yeah, right," Giblet harrumphed.

Before everyone left for their missions, Belle pulled Joel aside into a different bedroom so she could speak privately.

"Joel, I have a question for you...After everything we've learned, are you still feeling guilty about Oba's death?" she asked, looking into his eyes.

"What brings this up right now, young Missy?" Joel asked suspiciously.

"I know from seeing the Woman-Person's pictures that a cat named MacKayla was here when you came to live with our people. Also, Mittens has remarked that MacKayla was the wisest cat she ever knew, and you both were very close," Joel nodded but kept silent.

"I was wondering, what do you think MacKayla would say about you still blaming yourself?"

"Why do you want to know?" Joel responded, looking down at Belle apprehensively.

"Because Oba's death was not your fault. I think it's important that you understand that. Everything we have learned points out that it wouldn't have made a difference if you had been there."

Joel was quiet for a time and then smiled at Belle. "MacKayla would have liked you. You remind me of her sometimes. It's a shame you never met her." Belle smiled at the compliment but noticed Joel didn't answer the question.

From the hallway, Mittens called out, "Okay, cats. Time to go."

"I'll think about what you said, young Missy. I promise," with that, Joel licked her head and headed out into the hall.

Mittens and Joel left the house a little while later and climbed the mountain, heading toward Oba's old cabin. They walked in silence, Joel taking point and Mittens scanning the forest and listening.

They arrived at the old cabin and stopped; Joel sat down and stared bleakly at the ruin.

"Are you okay, Joel?"

"Yeah, I am," the old cat sighed. "I jus' had a good life here. At night, when I wus comin' home, I'd see tha windows lit by the kerosene lamps, an' smoke commin outa' the chimney. Oba would be setten on the porch, an we'd listen to the night.

"I'm sorry you lost this life," Mittens said, motioning to the cabin with a paw. "But if it's any consolation, we are blessed that you came into our lives."

Joel nodded, acknowledging the genuine warmth this family had for him.

"It's not too far ta go," Joel said, getting to his paws and stretching. "I wonder what's left in the Mine?"

He started off but came to a stop almost immediately. Mittens hadn't acknowledged his remarks. Turning around, he saw her standing, stock still, with her tail up and her eyes closed, concentrating intensely. Having lived with a Protector for the last ten years, he recognized that she sensed danger. Quietly, he got ready to attack or retreat.

"We can't go to the mine," Mittens said, opening her eyes. "We are being hunted," she said softly.

"Can ya tell who's trackin us?" Joel whispered.

"I know tracking, and I know hunting. We are being hunted." Mittens closed her eyes again and then announced, "It's a cat, and it feels like she has Protector training."

"How can ya tell she has the trainin', an' how do ya know it's a she?"

"I've smelled that cat before. The night Dolion paid the family a visit."

Mittens opened her eyes and looked at Joel, "It's Lucinda. I know how a Protector hunts when she needs to. Subtle characteristics make tracking different from hunting," she informed him. "Lucinda is hunting us."

Joel took the news without surprise. "I suspect she wants us to lead her to Oba's still an' then get rid of us." He added, "Dolion always wanted to know where it was."

Coming to a decision, Joel continued. "I gotta confession. She was the one who distracted me the day Oba was killed. That's why I couldn't warn him it was a trap. I never told anyone about that before. I felt ashamed."

"Joel, you have nothing to be ashamed about. You're a good cat." Then, changing the subject, she asked, "We haven't talked about Lucinda. What can you tell me about her? Where did she get Protector training?"

"She knows about being a Protector because this town used to have one until she killed em."

Mittens took in that news but didn't react. Instead, her mind was racing with scenarios and what tactics she would need if she confronted Lucinda.

"Lucinda could be charming. But, once you got to know her, you realized that the charm was only a tool to get what she wanted. That cat was always calculatin', tryin' bend any situation in her favor."

I was young, and I thought she liked me, so we hung out together sometimes," Joel admitted. "When we were together, I seen that she likes killing. She's gone outta her way to kill a mouse or bird because she likes it."

"Good to know," Mittens responded, filing away what she learned for later. "Let's circle around and head back to the house. I want to see how far she follows us." Together, both cats set off in a wide circle. Soon they were heading down slope, back towards town.

Lucinda knew she had been spotted when it became apparent they were heading back the way they came. Lucinda stopped hunting the pair and considered what to do next. *I won't underestimate this Protector again,* she thought. *But these two aren't the only ones I could get information from. Perhaps I will have better luck with the other two."*

When Jarred pulled up to the Police Station around 9:30 in the morning, Giblet and Belle were waiting. There was no doubt that this vehicle belonged to the Chief of Police since every flat area of the car had the word "Chief" in big, bold letters stenciled on it. Both cats figured Jarred must be worried that somebody would forget he was the chief.

Showing little concern for the "No Parking" signs or the fire hydrant, Jarred parked in the front of the station and walked in carrying a large cup of coffee and a bag from the local bakery.

"Cops and donuts. Talk about your tired cliché," Giblet observed.

"Also, he doesn't exactly follow the rules or get to work early, does he?" Belle observed from their hiding spot across the street, and Giblet nodded in agreement.

The Busby, West Virginia Police Station sat next door to city hall and the municipal courts building. The station was an older brick and stone building that looked like it was built in the early part of the last century when the town went through its building boom from coal money. The building's facade had "POLICE STATION" carved into the stone, and there were a pair of round glass carriage lights on either side of the doors with the word "POLICE."

The two cats moved around the back of the station and found where the rest of the cops and civilian employees parked their cars. While most of the windows were frosted glass and had bars across them, a few were clear.

"Keep an eye out and let me know if someone is coming. I'm going to peek in the windows," Belle said and scampered off before Giblet could raise an objection. *She's always doing that,* the tom cat grumbled. As he watched, Belle leaped up on the brick windowsill and looked in. After a minute, she returned.

"The window there on the corner is Jarred's office. He is in there, working at the computer, but I couldn't see the screen."

"Did you see anything else in the other windows?" Giblet asked.

"Just what looks like a break room and a hallway. Nothing we can use."

Glancing at the chief's car, she noticed Jarred had left the front windows open, giving Belle an idea. "I'm going to take a look in his car. You never know what People might leave out."

"He could come out at any moment. It's too dangerous," Giblet said firmly.

"You can warn me if he comes out, and I will only be a second. So quit worrying," she said with a smile and ran off to the car.

Belle hopped through the passenger window and looked around the front seat. Old candy wrappers and assorted trash littered the seat and floor, but there didn't appear to be anything of use. She jumped into the back seat to check it out; however, there wasn't anything useful there either, just more trash.

Well, this was a bust, she thought to herself and prepared to jump out of the window when she heard Giblet's howl. Before she could make good her escape, the driver's door opened and Jarred got in.

Without hesitation, she jumped to the car floor and wedged herself under the front passenger seat as far as she could. From under the seat, she continued to hear Giblet's howl and a much more disturbing sound of the engine starting. A few seconds later, the windows were up, and the car was moving. *"Oh, Poop,"* she thought.

Giblet took off at full-run and tried to follow Jarred's car but came to a stop after only a block. Watching the car speeding up and disappearing around a corner, he realized there was no chance he could keep up with it. *I have to get back to Mittens. She will know what to do,* he thought to himself, turning around and heading for home.

There was another set of eyes watching as Belle was whisked away. Lucinda saw Giblet give up his chase, turn and head in the direction of his home. *Well, isn't this interesting,* she thought, as she considered her options. Making a decision, Lucinda headed off in a different direction, a plan forming in her head.

Cat Time:
Ten Years Earlier – Torrington, CT

Ghost sat quietly as his new Person drove them to Connecticut. She was going to a meeting for something, but Ghost really didn't care. Finally, after a few hours, they pulled up to their destination, a white clapboard house in a town called Torrington.

He felt his carrier being lifted and brought into the house. An unfamiliar Man-Person and Woman-Person looked at him through the carrier's door and made a fuss about what a handsome cat he was.

"Put him up in the guest bedroom," Ghost heard the man say. "He can get used to the place, and it will give him a chance to meet our cat MacKayla."

"There's nothing to worry about," the Woman quickly reassured. "MacKayla gets along with everyone."

He was placed in the bedroom and left alone with the carrier door open. Ghost really didn't feel like investigating this new place, so he just stayed in the doorway of the carrier and closed his eyes.

Downstairs, the Man-Person and Woman-Person poured some tea for their guest, sat in the living room, and exchanged pleasantries. They talked about her drive from New York and the cat she'd brought with her. MacKayla came in and sat on the couch next to her People to listen to their conversation.

"I adopted Joel Grey a little over a month ago, but he really hasn't fit in. He doesn't hiss, scratch, or make any fuss. All he does all day is stare out the window. I don't think he's happy."

"Well, you said he was a stray. I wonder if he ever had a good home?" MacKayla heard her Woman-Person offer.

The conversation gradually transitioned to the reason for the visit. The Woman-Person excused herself, and the Man-Person started talking about her dissertation research. At that point, MacKayla got up and went upstairs to meet the Russian Blue visitor.

Coming into the bedroom, she saw Joel in his carrier and said cheerfully, "You must be the cat my People said was going to visit."

Ghost wasn't really sleeping and immediately heard a cat address him. He opened his eyes to see a tabby cat staring at him. "I'm MacKayla, by the way," she added matter-of-factly.

Ghost stared at the house cat without comment. She had a round face, white whiskers, and lovely markings around her eyes. She wasn't old, but she wasn't a young cat either, perhaps nine or ten human years of age, and on the smallish side with ears that pointed up and twitched back and forth. Her looks, combined with her cheerful personality, gave her an almost elfin appearance and an enduringly youthful quality.

When Ghost didn't reply, MacKayla meowed, "What's the matter? Cat got your tongue?" she asked with a twinkle in her eye. "What's your name?"

Seeing that his silence was unlikely to put her off, he decided to answer. "I'm Ghost," he said after a moment.

"I thought I heard the People call you Joel Grey?"

"That's what the Woman-Person who fetched us here is callin' me. I wus born and raised bein' called Grey Ghost."

Ahh, he had a prior Person, she thought to herself. "Your accent is not from around here. So, where are you from?" MacKayla asked, probing.

Why does everyone wonder where I am from? Ghost wondered. "I wus born an' raised in Busby, West Virginia," he said, hoping that this little cat would tire of asking questions. But no such luck; MacKayla continued with her friendly interrogation.

"That's certainly a long way from here. What's it like there?"

Ghost stared into the distance and said, "Mountains and forest everywhere. The smell of the earth, trees, and plants is different from here. Lots of good critters live there…and a few bad ones," he reminisced.

"Tell me about your home in Busby," MacKayla asked in a soft, compassionate voice.

"I had a couple of homes; one in town and a log cabin up on the Mountain. My Person an' I mostly stayed in the cabin."

"I've never seen a real log cabin before," MacKayla admitted. "Are they fun for cats?"

"Hell yeah," Ghost said, finally coming out of the carrier and sitting up.

"It had a big stone fireplace. An' if you came up in winter, you knew you wus getting' close because you'd smell the wood smoke from the chimney. So you'd hike a little further, an' then you'd see it, a little wood cabin nestled between the trees, all covered with fresh snow. There was a big front porch an' a couple of windows with warm lamp light spillin out onto the snow. Finally, you'd go inside, an' you'd lay on the rug in front of the fireplace, warmin your paws, while my Person cooked dinner for us.

I wus raised in tha cabin since I wus a kitten," Ghost added.

"It really sounds nice," MacKayla said, meaning it.

"Yeah. In the spring, you'd smell the forest as it come back alive, an' all the wildflowers growin naturally around. Then, at night, you'd hear the rain hit the wood shingles on the roof. It was a cozy spot, a good home," Joel said, enjoying the memory.

One of MacKayla's gifts was being able to read emotions in others. Her incredible empathic abilities were unmeasurable. She could read how a Person, cat, or other animal felt as though it were written across their face. It was what made her such a good housecat for her People. She could see when they were having a bad day and would make a special effort to help them.

"Why did you leave?" she asked softly. Instead of answering right away, Ghost got a pained look on his face. *Ahh, that's the key,* MacKayla thought. *Why he left?*

MacKayla mentally discarded the next question she was going to ask and instead played a hunch and asked, "Your Person died, didn't he?"

Ghost didn't answer. Instead, he took a deep breath and looked away.

"You know, the quickest way to get over pain is to accept it," MacKayla said compassionately.

Still, Ghost remained silent and wouldn't meet MacKayla's eyes. Moving closer, she reached out her paw and patted him gently.

"He died," Ghost finally said aloud for the first time. Then his eyes welled up, and he began to cry.

CHAPTER XIII

From Bad To Worse

A soft, sinister voice meowed in her ear,
"Keep still, little Protector, or you're dead."

Cat Time:
Unknown

Belle stayed hidden under the seat while Jarred drove around, wondering if he was ever going to stop long enough for her to escape. She stuck her head out a couple of times but couldn't tell where she was from the backseat floor of the patrol car. All she could see from her angle was the sky. Jarred made several stops during their drive; each time, he kept the windows up, leaving Belle trapped.

After each stop, Jarred would return to the car with a paper sack and dump a wad of People money on the front seat. Belle would watch his reflection in the car window as he counted the money. She also heard him count aloud like the children did with their schoolwork. Unfortunately, Jarred made several tallying mistakes and had to start over each time. It appeared that the chief of police of Busby, West Virginia, was not great at math.

One of these stops, I am just going to have to run for it, Belle thought. *I can't afford to be trapped in here all night. Giblet will have a heart attack.*

At about the same time, an out-of-breath Giblet arrived back home. Bursting into the house, he meowed loudly, "MITTENS!...WHERE'S MITTENS?" Then a second later, "MITTENS, I NEED YOU!"

A moment later, Mittens, Joel, and even Iko came rushing into the kitchen in answer to Giblet's cries. All three animals peppered him with questions simultaneously, asking what was wrong.

"It's Belle! She's trapped! We have to find her!" Giblet meowed as he paced quickly around the room.

Mittens held up her paw to silence Joel and Iko and then turned to the clearly agitated Giblet, "Slow down. Start at the beginning. Where is Belle?"

"We went to the police station to check on Jarred, you know, to see what we could find out," he said in a rush. "She wanted to check out his car. I didn't want her to, but she wouldn't listen. She jumped in through the window, but before she could get out, he drove away with her inside. We have to find her!"

"Giblet...Giblet, look at me," Mittens insisted, trying to calm down the large tabby cat. "Belle is smart; she won't panic. Do you think Jarred knows that Belle was in the car?"

"I don't know. I called out a warning before Jarred got into the car."

"Did Belle have enough time to hide?" Joel asked. "Before he got in?"

"I don't know...maybe," Giblet answered, feeling a glimmer of hope.

"Do you know where Jarred lives?" Mittens asked Joel.

"Yeah. But that wus ten years ago," the old grey cat admitted.

"It's a place to start," Mittens said aloud. Then coming to a quick decision, she added, "Joel and I will go over to Jarred's house and check it out." Then turning to Giblet, she said, "I want you to stay here in case she escapes and comes home. Anne is still out with the People-Kittens; I need you to fill her in on what is going on.

Seeing how upset he was, Mittens put her paw on Giblet's shoulder and said, "It's going to be okay, Giblet. Belle is very capable, and Jarred is an idiot. More than likely, he will never know she is along for the ride."

Iko, I need you to stay with Giblet and keep him company," the dog wagged her tail in agreement.

Giblet looked at her with pain in his eyes and nodded while Iko came over and sat next to him. Even though he was not a huge fan of dogs, Giblet sincerely appreciated the gesture.

With orders given and a plan set, Mittens and Joel left while Giblet sat next to Iko, a silent prayer to the Great Cat in the Sky going over and over in his head.

"If he hurts her, I'm gonna kill him," Joel said aloud as he and Mittens made their way to Jarred's home. Mittens didn't say anything, knowing he was just blowing off steam. But she knew that she would also exact retribution if Jarred hurt Belle.

According to Joel, when last he knew, Jarred lived in an old apartment on the edge of Busby. The area, he had commented, was not a nice neighborhood.

They made good time, with Joel keeping up a quick pace, despite his age. His grim determination helping him overcome his aching joints. Soon, they came upon a seedy apartment complex of a half-dozen units. Several People sat in lawn chairs by their front doors and gossiped back and forth while a few People-Kittens played on broken playground equipment. Weeds poking up through cracks in the parking lot and sidewalks completed the unpleasant picture. The complex looked like it hadn't had much in the way of upkeep or care for a long time.

"This complex was owned by Dolion's family when I lived here. From the looks of it, they probably still own it," Joel commented.

"Which unit is Jarred's?" Mittens asked quietly.

"The one on the end, with the broken screen door," came the response.

"I don't see his police car around. Do you think he is still at work?"

"Probably. It ain't quittin' time, I reckon," Joel guessed.

They made their way to the end unit, and Mittens said she would jump up to the side window and take a look. Joel nodded and signaled he would keep watch. The senior Protector leaped gracefully onto the windowsill and looked inside. Then, after about ten seconds, she jumped back down and returned to Joel.

"Does Jarred have a family?" she asked.

"He didn't when I knew him. What did ya see?"

"There was a woman in the kitchen with a small child in a playpen. Both look pretty young," Mittens observed. "Let's see if we can find someone who can tell us who lives there."

They looked around the apartment complex, trying to find some animal to corroborate who lived in the end unit. Finally, after a few cat minutes, they came across a one-eyed tuxedo cat who appeared to be arguing with a white rat about politics.

"…You're crazy. I can see it clearer than you even with one eye," the tuxedo cat remarked.

"You cats, all high and mighty. Try living as a rat for a while, and you will know…" the rat responded.

"Excuse me," Mittens interrupted. "Do either of you know who lives in that end apartment?" she pointed with her paw.

"Who are you?" the white rat asked, sitting up on his back legs and giving the pair of cats a good once-over.

"I'm Mittens, and this is Joel Grey," she answered. "We are searching for a friend of ours. She is a smallish back cat, and her name is Belle."

"The Riley's live in that unit," the tuxedo replied. "Have been since I've been around here; going on five cat years now."

"Do ya know where Jarred, the police chief, lives?" Joel asked.

Both animals shook their head and said "no."

"I would really appreciate it if you would keep—" Mittens was going to say *an eye out* but decided instead to say, "—An ear out for our friend,

Belle. She's missing. We are staying at the white, two-story clapboard house on Maple Street."

Both animals said they would be on the lookout for Belle. Then the tuxedo, his one eye narrowing at Mittens, said, "You're a Protector, ain't you." It came out as a statement, not a question.

"Yes," Mittens answered. "How did you know?"

"I heard other cats talk about them. It's the cattitude that I sense from you."

"Do you have a Protector for this area?" Joel asked.

"No, we had one years ago, I was told. But another cat killed her in a fight."

Joel raised his eyebrow at this but kept quiet.

"Are you going to be our new Protector?" the rat asked, a tinge of hope in his voice.

"No. I'm sorry. My People family and I are only in town for the summer," Mittens said.

"That's too bad. We will look around for your friend," the tuxedo promised. "I hope she comes home safe."

Joel and Mittens thanked them and started heading back in the general direction of the center of town. Without a better idea of where Belle might be, they decided that starting at the police station was as good a place as any.

Jarred pulled up to his house after a long day of collecting money for Dolion. All he wanted to do was to watch television and have a beer. But, no sooner had he turned off the engine than a large animal landed on his hood with a loud thump and meowed loudly at him through the windshield.

Getting over his initial shock, he recognized the animal well enough; it was Dolion's cat Lucinda, and she had about scared him half to death.

Belle also heard the meow from under the seat and recognized it immediately. It was the same caterwaul as the other night when Lucinda had growled and hissed at the Children. *As soon as he opens the door, I'm outta here,* she thought. *That old cat will never be able to keep up with me.*

"What the hell are you doing, Lucinda? Get off my car," Jarred screamed as he opened the car door. However, before he could step out, Lucinda jumped in through the open door and then into the back seat. Then, from the car's back seat, Jarred heard one heck of a catfight.

Belle had crawled from under the seat and was preparing to jump out of the car as fast as she could when a sudden and unfamiliar weight landed on her, knocking the wind out of her lungs. A loud, angry growl and hiss filled Belle's ears; all at once, she knew this fight was deadly serious.

In a testament to her Protector training, she recovered quickly and set her rear paws to push her body up and throw off the attacker. If done right, the move would end up with Belle on her back, with her front and back paws free to counterattack. However, as soon as she started to get ready, the rear claws of her attacker dug into her back hips, effectively stopping her from employing the counter move.

Belle wasn't finished, however. Instead, she started to use her superior flexibility to reach her head around to bite the paw holding down her right shoulder. As soon as that weight was lifted, she could reach up and use her front claws.

Just as she turned her head, a pair of powerful jaws clamped down on her neck, at the base of her skull. The attacker's mandibles began to close with incredible power when she wiggled ever so slightly. This was no play wrestling move like she would perform with Giblet; the pressure on her spine stopped her cold. Belle knew instantly that this cat could snap her neck if she wished.

Evaluate the situation and plan your next move; Mittens had constantly drilled into her during her training. So, Belle kept her head perfectly still and relaxed, letting the tension drain from her body. However, that didn't prevent her from letting out a long, angry hiss.

A soft and sinister voice meowed in her ear, "Keep still, little Protector, or you're dead." Lucinda felt the small black cat relax but ignored it. She didn't discount the abilities of any animal when they were fighting for their life.

Jarred had finally gotten out of the car and opened the rear door to see what all the fuss was about. He saw Lucinda holding down a smaller, black cat on the back seat floor. "How'd that cat get in here," he asked aloud to no one in particular.

Belle remained motionless but continued to hiss. Lucinda also growled. A moment later, Belle felt the weight coming off her back, but then a strong, cold pair of hands grabbed her by the scruff of the neck and back.

As she was lifted out of the car, Belle saw Lucinda staring at her from the back seat, keeping an eye on her, and she saw Jarred up close for the first time. She wasn't impressed.

"What are we gonna do with you?" the police chief asked, looking around. Lucinda growled instructions, but Jarred, of course, had no idea she was saying anything.

However, Belle knew exactly what Lucinda had said. "If he lets you go, little Protector, you're mine. But if he doesn't, that will also work," she meowed. For her part, Belle remained quiet, turning her head back and forth, looking for any opportunity.

Not sure what to do, Jarred carried Belle over to the side of the house, opened the cellar doors, and tossed the black cat in; then, he shut the doors quickly so she couldn't escape. He didn't want a cat, but his boss seemed to like them. He would mention finding this cat to Dolion later and see if he had any suggestions.

Looking back at Lucinda, sitting on the roof of the car and watching him, he wondered aloud, "How'd you know that little cat was in the car?" Then, not expecting an answer, he closed up his car and walked to his front door. But, before entering the house, he glared at Lucinda and said, "Git outta here."

Lucinda didn't move until Jarred was inside, then she went around to the back of the house.

Belle had landed on her feet on a dirt floor and heard the cellar doors slam shut behind her. Collecting herself, she walked up to the cellar doors and tentatively pushed against them; either they were locked or much too heavy for her to lift. *Of course not,* she thought. *That would have made things much too easy.*

Walking back down to the dirt floor, she took account of her impromptu cell. The cellar was roughly square, and the walls were built out of stone and showed their age. A large, rusty old furnace was sitting on a small concrete pad in the center, and a few shelves were running along one wall. A solitary light with a string attached to it hung near the furnace. Belle figured the string turned the light on and off; *good to know,* she thought. There were two ground-level windows along one wall, looking out into what must be the backyard. One of the windows had bars across it, but the other did not.

Belle walked over and jumped up to the sill of the unbarred window, only to come whisker to whisker with Lucinda on the other side of the glass.

"Going somewhere, little Protector?" the cat meowed at her with a grin. Belle thought *this cat doesn't smile much, and when she does, it's for the wrong reasons.*

Belle had no problem hearing Lucinda through the glass but did not answer immediately. Instead, she took time to study the window with a critical eye. Unfortunately, the window was shut tight, with a lock of a type that Belle had not seen before. *That's a problem,* she thought to herself.

Finally, she turned her complete attention to Lucinda and took a good, long look. She was a large Persian, not quite as big as Mittens. She guessed the Persian's age to be younger than Joel, maybe about the same age as Mittens. She was powerfully built, and when you got close, you could see there were deep scars on her face and crisscrossing on her chest, probably from fights with other animals. But the eyes gave Belle the most information; cold, cruel eyes without compassion. The eyes screamed, "Killer."

"Well, you stay safe," Lucinda purred. "I have a distillery to find, and your buddy Ghost is going to lead me to it. But, of course, that is if he wants to see you alive again."

"I'm not worried," Belle said, speaking for the first time in a calm voice. "When you meet Mittens, you are going to regret doing this," she responded with bravado, meaning it. "Protectors have no sense of humor concerning matters like this."

Lucinda got a wicked smile on her face that made her seem to radiate evil. "I'm not worried. She wouldn't be the first Protector I've killed." Then with a swish of her tail, she ran off.

Belle sat and considered what Lucinda had told her. *"Well, poop, again,"* The young Protector thought.

Cat Time:
Ten Years Earlier, Torrington, CT

For the next week, Ghost (or Joel, depending on whom you asked) spent all of his time with MacKayla. They would sit in the window, watch birds, and talk to each other. Ghost told her about Busby and how Obadiah had found him as a tiny kitten, so small that he had to be bottle-fed. Next, he told her about whiskey-making and some of their adventures together. Then, after a couple of days, he felt secure enough to reveal how Oba had died and that he should have been there but was distracted by Lucinda, a cat he thought he could trust.

MacKayla told Ghost about her life and being adopted as a kitten by the young couple. She told him how the couple had been trying to have People-Kittens for the last few years and how she would care for them and make them feel better after each setback. "All in all, I have had a good life with these People," she purred.

MacKayla listened as Ghost poured his heart out. Then, after hearing the whole story, she told him it wasn't his fault that Oba was shot. "Bad people are going to do bad things. But, for the most part, cats can't stop the evil in the world; not even a Protector," she said compassionately.

"Knowing him the way you did, do you think Oba would blame you?" she asked.

"Probably not, but I blame me," was his reply.

MacKayla let the matter rest. It would take him time to come to grips with the past, and dwelling on it wouldn't help. So instead, she took him around the house, showed him all the best bird-watching windows, and then took him to meet the grandparents who lived with them. The grandfather took an immediate liking to Joel and let him sit on his lap in the evenings.

The grandfather didn't smell like wood smoke, whiskey, or the forest. Still, there was something familiar about sitting on the Old-Person's lap, listening to him talk—something recognizable and comforting.

In a couple of days, Ghost's new Person would finish her meetings at the university, and they would be heading back to New York. Although the weight on his shoulders had lessened considerably during the visit, it was not gone. Joel had grown close to MacKayla during their time together, and he worried about what he would do if she weren't around to listen to him. That thought lingered in his mind as he went to sleep next to his new friend.

CHAPTER XIV

The Confinement

Great, Belle mumbled to herself. *Another year, another house, and I am in another darn furnace duct.*

Cat Time:
The Full Rose Moon

Mittens and Joel staked out the police station until well after dark but Jarred never returned. Without any better ideas, they decided to return home to see if Belle had returned on her own. Unfortunately, the news was not great when they finally arrived.

A clearly anxious Giblet and Iko met them as soon as they entered the house. When they saw that Belle was not with them, Iko hung her head, and Giblet began pacing back and forth, getting more worked up by the second.

"Giblet, look at me," Mittens instructed. "Stand still and focus on me; we will find Belle. But first, you need to tell me what has been happening here while we were out. It's important."

"When Anne got home with the People-Kittens, I told her everything that has been going on. She is worried but couldn't do anything as long as she had to watch the People-Kittens," Giblet said in a rush. "The Man-Person and Woman-Person got home and noticed we were three cats short. I did my best to distract them. But they wondered where the rest of you were."

"Did Anne cover for us?" Joel asked.

"She said you might be sleeping in the basement or somewhere in the house. She covered for you two as best she could."

Turning to Joel, Mittens said, "Let's go and make an appearance. We can't have the family getting too suspicious." Iko and the three cats agreed and went into the family room and hung out with the family until they went to bed. The cats tried to act as normal as possible, but Giblet and Joel were restless and couldn't settle on a lap for any length of time. The Woman-Person noticed the agitation.

"The cats seem skittish tonight," Shirley noted as Giblet left her lap for the fourth time that evening.

"I bet it's a full moon tonight," Anne suggested, looking up from her book. "Animals are always different during a full moon."

Across the room, Mittens caught Giblet's eye and glared at him. Her frown was quite clear to the tabby cat—*settle down, or the People will become suspicious.*

"It's not the moon that affects the animals," the Man-Person offered, looking up from his laptop. "It's the light. A full moon is ten times brighter than even a half moon. Therefore, it causes more nocturnal activity."

"About the only nocturnal activity I'm interested in right now is bed," the Woman-Person announced, rising to her feet.

"I will be right along. I just need to finish these notes from today," the Man-Person replied.

Finally, everyone was in bed and asleep. Anne, the cats, Iko, and Porter met on the front porch. Porter was brought up to speed on Belle's disappearance and the unsuccessful search for Jarred's new house.

"Do you know where Jarred lives?" Giblet asked the Highland Collie.

"Ah dinnae ken," Porter responded with a sad face. "Hae moved awhile agoo."

"FOR CAT'S SAKE," Giblet howled, getting in Porter's face. "You live here; how could you not know where he lives?"

Porter was a reasonably easygoing Highlander, except when someone questioned his loyalty…or they were getting in his face.

"Haud yer wheesht!" He woofed back at Giblet. "Ah worried about the wee bairn, same as ye."

Giblet wasn't sure precisely what Porter said, but from the context and the glare on the Highland Collie's face, he guessed he was told to be quiet and not necessarily politely.

"Arguing among ourselves is not going to accomplish anything," Mittens responded with her stern, Protector's voice. "Porter, do you know anyone who might know where the Jarred moved?"

Porter shook his head no. The rest of them stayed quiet and tried to come up with an answer.

"The police department doesn't generally release the addresses of cops, and certainly not chiefs," Anne contributed. "That is a good way to get a cop killed."

"Okay. Here is what we are going to do. If Belle isn't home by tomorrow morning, Giblet and I will go to the police station early and wait for Jarred to arrive." She looked at Giblet, and he nodded. "Joel, I want you and Porter to return to where Jarred last lived. See if that tuxedo cat we talked to found out anything useful." Joel and Porter both nodded in agreement.

"I will be up to your place in the mornin'," Joel said. "Y'all wait fur me there, and we will git goin'." Porter woofed in agreement.

Finally, she turned to Anne, "I would appreciate it if you stayed here in case Belle shows back up."

"The kids and I were going to the library in the afternoon, but we can be here until you get back," Anne confirmed.

Iko listened to the back and forth between the animals and Anne, and she desperately wanted to help search for Belle. Of all the cats, she was closest to that little black cat and felt a strong protective instinct toward her. She looked at Mittens and woofed, "I want to go with you tomorrow. You need me."

Mittens saw that Iko wanted to be included, but she worried that a dog along with them would attract too much attention. "Iko, I need you to stay here. We need someone we trust to be at the house if Belle comes back while everyone has gone."

"But—," Iko began to say but then stopped. Everyone, People, cats, and the dog, was on edge, and she didn't want to upset anyone further. So instead, she swallowed what she was going to say and nodded in agreement.

"Good. Thank you," Mittens replied, knowing Iko wanted to argue the point. "Look, I know it isn't going to be easy to sleep, but we will need all our strength tomorrow. So, let's put our heads down and try to rest. Belle is a very smart and very capable cat. Right now, I'll bet she is planning her escape or is waiting, knowing we will rescue her."

Rising to her paws, Mittens took a long breath and said, "Besides, I have found that the most vexing problem can usually be solved if you are patient. So we need to be patient now, more than ever…Agreed?"

Everyone woofed, meowed, and nodded in agreement.

"See you all tomorrow morning, early,"

Porter walked over to Giblet and licked his head once, letting him know he didn't take their dust-up personally. Giblet nodded and appreciated the gesture. After that, Anne went off to bed, and Mittens started to the master bedroom but stopped and looked behind her.

"Coming, Joel?" she meowed.

"Sure enough," he said. I jus' gonna sit here for a minute and see if the little scamp shows up."

"I'll sit with him," Giblet offered.

"Okay," Mittens replied.

Joel settled on the porch and listened to the night with Giblet next to him, but he had no intentions of waiting until morning. He knew there was one cat who would know where Jarred lived and might even know where Belle was. And he was damned if he was going to wait for morning to find out. As soon as Giblet was asleep, he would find Lucinda and get the truth…or die trying.

Great, Belle mumbled to herself. Another year, another house, and I am in another darn furnace duct. If the Protector job doesn't work out, I could probably get a job as an official furnace duct inspector, her grim humor an attempt to lighten the mood.

Several hours before, as she was being carried to the cellar by Jarred, Belle squirmed in his hands. She was trying to get away, but she was also trying to see as much of the house and surrounding area as possible.

Sitting in the basement as night fell, she went over the details of what she saw in her mind. It appeared to be a single-story, older, clapboard house in desperate need of a paint job. There were woods along the back of the house, and she could just make out a road running past the front. The cellar door was on the right side by the driveway. She couldn't turn her head enough to see if there were any other houses nearby before she was dumped, unceremoniously, into her cell.

After Lucinda left, she explored where she was in detail. The most apparent thing was that there were no steps into the house from the cellar. From her reading, she knew People had to go outside to get to the cellar in many older southern homes. Steps going down into a basement was a northern house tradition.

She noted that there was a massive old furnace in the basement, with ducts that came off a central main and probably went into each room for heat. Next to the furnace was a rusty water heater; its pipes went to what Belle guessed were a bathroom and a kitchen.

But the most intriguing thing was that the central duct appeared to have an opening for warm air to blow into the cellar onto the water heater, probably a precaution against freezing pipes in the winter. Racking her brain, she remembered that the heating registers in the Torrington house did not fasten down to the floor; they were simply set in the duct opening, and their weight kept them in place. This gave Belle an idea.

If I crawl into the duct and find a register, I should be able to push it up and escape. Thank Cat, I'm not the size of Giblet or Joel, then I'd never fit. The alternative was to sit and wait for Jarred and Lucinda to return. What they might end up doing with her was not pleasant to consider.

For the next several minutes, she studied the pipes and ductwork. As she stared at the furnace, she knew the front of the house was to her left, which would be the main room, and the back was to her right. *Over there should be the kitchen, and over there should be a bathroom based on the water and drainpipes. The two ducts over here,* she thought, turning her head, *should lead to the bedrooms.*

When she was finished mapping out the house's rooms as best she could, she listened to the activity above her. *It's still early, and I hear a television on, so Jarred should be in the front room.*

She knew that if she jumped on the water heater and crossed over to the furnace, she could stretch up just enough to reach the central duct opening. From there, it was a right turn and straight until she could feel a gap on her left. That should be the duct that leads to a bedroom. "If I can't lift the register, I will back up and retrace my steps back to this opening," she said aloud to muster her courage. "Not an ideal situation, but doable."

"Well, it's now or never," Belle meowed softly and leaped onto the water heater to begin her journey. Soon, she was in the duct, pointed in the direction that she hoped would lead to her escape. If the ducts in the Torrington house were dirty, these were even worse; it was filthy. Belle was soon covered in years of dust, lint, and other substances that it was best not to dwell on.

It's summer, she thought. *At least I don't have to worry about the furnace turning on.*

Feeling along with her paws, she found the passage on her left that, by her calculations, should lead to the bedroom. She made her way along slowly. Unfortunately, compared to last year, she was no longer the tiny kitten she once was. The muscle she had put on had advantages and disadvantages in situations like this. *I can still make it through, but this is going to be tight,* she thought.

From the cellar floor, she calculated that the distance she would have to go in the smallest duct was about six feet to reach the end. But inside the cramped, pitch-black duct, it felt like she crawled forever. Then, finally, she could see some light filtering down from the register.

She got under the register grate and very slowly pushed it up with her head. *Please, please, please...don't be fastened down,* she prayed to the great Cat in the sky, and to her joy, the grate began to lift.

As her head with the register resting on it slowly rose above the floor level, she could see that she was not in an empty bedroom but what looked more like a small office. She had a view of an old desk and the legs of a chair. But, worst of all, someone was sitting in the chair, and that pair of legs had to belong to Jarred.

Oh, my CAT, when am I going to catch a break?

CHAPTER XV

The Ransome Demand

"Hey Ghost, come here, you little rascal.
Let's go make some whiskey."

Cat Time:
The Full Rose Moon, continued

Joel crept out of the house when he was sure Giblet and the People were asleep. Then, cautiously, he made his way to Dolion's house with confrontation on his mind. He knew in his heart that Lucinda had something to do with Belle not making it home, and he would get his answers from her.

Walking through Busby these last few days triggered so many powerful memories for Joel that he felt overwhelmed. Thinking back, he had no recollection of his mother. His first memory was being bottle-fed in the little cabin on the mountain. When he was older, Oba had told Ghost how he was found.

"I wus in town, buyin' supplies at the general store when I came out an' heard you," Oba explained to Ghost. "I wus walkin' to my truck when I heard the faintest little squeak commin from between a couple of cars."

Oba had followed those soft meows and came upon a tiny grey kitten, all alone and crying.

Oba couldn't turn his back on any animal in need any more than he could stop breathing. Reaching down, he scooped up the little fur-ball in his large, calloused hand. The kitten was so tiny that it fit entirely in his palm. Examining his find, he guessed that the kitten was only days old; its eyes were open, but it weighed next to nothing.

"One thing was for sure and for certain, you were far too small to be on your own. And I could tell by your cries you needed to be fed," he had told Ghost.

"Did you ever find my mama?" Ghost had asked Oba during these story times.

"I looked, but I couldn't find a trace of her. So I put ya' in my jacket pocket, and we headed back to the cabin where I had feedin' supplies on hand. I liked to take care of animals I find on the mountain that needs help, an' that day, it was you," Oba said with a warm smile.

Ghost had always held onto that story from Oba. It showed the best of the man and his kindness.

The first thing Ghost actually remembered from that time was being in a strange room that looked like it was made out of logs. He was curled up in a towel on a warm lap and was sucking delicious milk from a tiny nipple. While he ate, he looked at the man with fur on his face and kind eyes, smiling down at him.

Oba made sure to feed the new arrival regularly, every two to four hours for the first week, then about four to five times a day for the next month. During mealtime, Oba began calling the kitten a little rascal.

Newborn kittens sleep most of the time, but as they grow and put on weight, their curiosity compels them to want to explore their surroundings. Ghost found out the place he was in was called a cabin and that he was called a cat; this information was provided by an old coon dog named Duke. The dog would let him curl up next to him for warmth and told him that the kind man taking care of him was Obadiah, Oba for short.

One of Ghost's favorite kitten games was to hide and pop out to surprise Oba. "Doggone it, you appear outta nowhere, like a little grey ghost." After a while, Oba began calling him the Grey Ghost, or Ghost for short. Even though he'd answered to the name of Joel for the last ten years, he would always be Ghost in his heart.

One day, Oba called out, "Hey Ghost, come here, you little rascal. Let's go make some whiskey." Of course, Ghost didn't know what that meant, but he was excited to be included. So, Oba scooped him up, called Duke over, and the three of them hiked up the mountain. Pretty soon, they arrived at the mine, and Ghost began his new career helping Oba make his famous whiskey.

Ghost soon became a watch-cat for the operation and was in charge of rodent control. He learned that a good mash had a strong, sharp yeasty smell, and a flawed mash had a pungent, vomit smell unless you were doing a sour-mash run. He learned about grains, yeast, distilling, and aging the whiskey; he even knew Oba's secret recipe.

After a couple of years, old Duke couldn't make the trek up the mountain any longer, so it was up to Ghost to accompany Oba on distilling days. Then, one day, Oba surprised Ghost with his name on the old still, calling him a "proprietor." It was one of the happiest times of Ghost's young life.

Ghost loved his life with Obadiah, who let him have the run of the mountain. He would often be out all day, exploring the forest and the community of Busby. Several shop owners knew Ghost was Oba's cat, and because they loved Oba's whiskey, they would give him treats when he visited.

Old age finally caught up to Duke, and he passed over the Rainbow Bridge. Ghost would always treasure the memory of the big coon dog, both his wisdom and his kindness.

Ghost thought the good times with Oba would never end. That was until Dolion Dubghall came on the scene. The only thing Ghost knew about this Person was what he heard Oba mutter. "He's the spoiled rotten, dishonest son of the town mortician."

Most of what passed for upper-class citizens of Busby didn't associate with the Dubghall family. Instead, they shunned the family unless they needed their services as morticians, and even then, those who could afford it went over to the next community.

"They're a bunch of strange ducks," most people in town would say. The father was cold and dour, and the mother was constantly bedridden with one ailment or another. Their only son, Dolion, was a perpetual brat as a child and was eventually sent off to boarding school. However, since they were the only funeral home in town, a significant portion of the population would require their services sooner or later. That steady stream of business ensured that the Dubghalls were one of Busby's wealthiest families.

The funeral home profits also allowed the Dubghalls to expand their family's influence. When young Dolion returned from college, he began working for the family business. Eventually, Dolion gained total control when his father became senile, and his mother never left her bed. One of Dolion's first purchases was the apartment complex he and Mittens had visited the day before.

High rent and low upkeep were the hallmarks of a Dubghall property. Dolion never spent a dime he didn't have to, and that sentiment extended to his own family. When his parents passed, Dolion put them in the plainest pine box he could find and dumped them into a single pauper's grave, stacking the coffins one on top of the other.

"When it's my time to go," Oba would say with a smile, "Jus' put me someplace on my mountain." Ghost thought of Obadiah's wishes and hoped his spirit was at rest on the mountain he loved so much.

Oba didn't associate with Dolion or his family, and Dolion would never have dreamed of associating himself with mountainfolk like Oba. However, when Dolion got into the moonshine business, it guaranteed that Oba and he would be on a collision course.

A year before Oba died, Dolion brought home a white Persian cat. She was large, as big as Ghost himself; Lucinda was her name. In the beginning, Lucinda ingratiated herself with the local animal population;

even the old Protector of the town liked her and began training her, perhaps to one day be her replacement.

Lucinda certainly stood out in a town of average-looking dogs and house cats. She would strut around and swish her tail back and forth under the noses of tom-cats and dogs; she liked to be noticed. Eventually, she and Ghost crossed paths.

One day, Oba and Ghost came into town on some errands. Oba was driving his battered old pickup, and Ghost was sitting in the passenger seat. As they passed the town park, Oba pointed and said, "Hey Ghost, ever seen a cat like that before?"

Ghost looked over to where Oba was pointing and saw a large white cat sitting in the gazebo of the town square.

While Oba took care of his business, Ghost padded over to meet Busby's newest resident. "You're new around here, ain't ya?" he purred at the white cat.

She smiled, got up, and circled Ghost, swishing her tail under his nose. "I'm Lucinda," she purred at him. That was it; Ghost was hooked. After their initial meeting, they began hanging out together all over town; they were the talk of the animal community.

Lucinda told Ghost that she was from a breeder several states away and that Dolion adopted her because he wanted a cat of "quality." Even though Ghost had a generally negative attitude toward Dolion, based on what Oba said, he thought Lucinda was a good cat. Besides, he also thought she had feelings for him. Thinking back, he was amazed at how wrong he was about everything.

After a few months, Ghost began noticing behavior in Lucinda that bothered him. For example, she would sometimes go out of her way to hunt a squirrel, mouse, or bird and kill it, not for food but because she thought it was fun. In addition, she began looking down her nose at the other animals in Busby. "They're not quality," she would say.

The Children of Busby knew better than to approach Lucinda. Word spread quickly that she would spit and hiss at any Child that wanted to pet her, whereas Ghost would welcome People-Kittens and let them pet him anytime.

Other animals in Busby noticed this behavior and cooled in their friendship with the white Persian; even Ghost eventually mentioned that her new behavior was bothering him.

"My human and I are going to run this town, Ghost," she said, shaking her paw at him. "You need to be on the right team. The winning team." Ghost stared at her and shook his head, wondering if this was the same cat he had first met.

Ghost knew Dolion had begun approaching other moonshiners and making deals with them. Some of the other distillers approached Oba, asking if he was going to partner with Dolion. He would always give the unambiguous answer, "NO!" Other distillers would remark they could actually hear the capital letters in Oba's response.

After that, Ghost stopped seeing Lucinda and made it a point to avoid her. *Perhaps she will come to her senses,* he hoped. However, that hope for a renewed relationship was destroyed when Lucinda murdered the only Protector Busby ever had.

It was a warm day in June when Oba and Ghost came to town for supplies. As they drove through town, Ghost noticed many animals were watching them, and a few even took off running when Ghost looked back at them. Being a People, Oba didn't sense the anxiety. As soon as they arrived at the General Store, Oba went in to do his shopping while Ghost approached a couple of cats he saw. But before he could meow a greeting, both cats turned tails and ran.

"Well, that was weird," Joel said aloud, not understanding why the cats took off so fast. Then, hearing some animal conversation from behind the store, he walked around and found a local dog and raccoon having a discussion. They didn't run off like the cats, but both eyed him cautiously.

"What in tarnation is goin' on?" Joel asked

"You didn't hear?" the dog asked. "The Protector was killed last night."

"I've been up on the mountain with Oba. I haven't heard nuthin," Ghost admitted.

"The Protector really put up a good fight," the raccoon said. "If she was a few years younger, I bet she would have won."

"You could hear that fight blocks away," the dog confided. "People were looking out their windows and doors tryin' to see where all the hissing and howling was coming from."

"Do you know what the fight was about?" Ghost asked.

"The Protector tried to stop another cat from killing some critter," the raccoon answered. "But when she intervened, the big white cat turned on her."

At the mention of a white cat, Ghost's face fell. "Do ya know who done the killing?" he asked, already knowing and dreading the answer.

"Yeah, it was that cat who belongs to the Mortician's son," the dog said. "Your friend, Lucinda."

"Lucinda is her name, all right," the raccoon confirmed. "Most of the animal population is afraid of her. They think the two of you are in cahoots."

"She's not my friend, not anymore. An' I certainly don't cotton to hurtin' other animals. That's why them cats left when I walked up," Ghost speculated.

"Yeah, that may be," the dog agreed. "But if you see her, you need to talk some sense into her, no matter what."

The dog and raccoon excused themselves and left as Ghost set out to find Lucinda. She was at the gazebo in the town square, her usual haunt, attempting to clean herself.

As he approached, he got a good look at her, and quite frankly, she was a mess, he thought. There were deep scratch marks on her face and bite marks on one ear. Dried blood was speckling her fur, and she seemed in pain on her left side. But, even after all that, she looked happy with herself.

"Why'd ya do it?" Ghost asked when he got close.

"Nobody is going to tell me what I can and can't do," Lucinda said arrogantly. "This is my town. Two and four-legged animals better realize that. You could have been by my side. We could run the animals of this town, but you made a mistake."

Ghost could see there was no point in trying to talk sense to her; the cat he thought he knew was gone. *I wonder if she ever really existed?* He thought silently.

"Bye, Lucinda," he finally said and began walking away. He still remembered her parting taunt of *"You'll be sorry!"*

After that, he never spoke to her again until that faithful day Oba died.

He and Oba had finished their deliveries before Thanksgiving, and Ghost was on his way to watch the football practice for the big game, but he never made it. Halfway there, one of the town cats told him that Lucinda needed to speak to him urgently.

"What's she want to talk to me about?" he asked the orange tabby.

"I don't know," the cat said, shaking his head. "But she's at the gazebo in the town square, and she says it's urgent."

Ghost was naturally suspicious, and the town square was in the opposite direction, across town, but his curiosity got the better of him. He found her waiting like he was told, a smug expression on her face.

"What'd you want, Lucinda?" Ghost asked, without preamble.

"I want to offer you a job," the white Persian said. "I want you to work for me."

"I got a job. Oba and I don't want anything to do with you or Dolion."

"Yeah, about that. I wouldn't count on Obadiah being an independent moonshiner in the future. I think he will be working for Dolion after today…after he heals up."

Ghost stared hard at her, his mind working overtime, trying to decipher what she was saying. Then, after a moment, realization dawned on him. They were after Oba, and he was being distracted. Looking at Lucinda, she nodded, smiling her evil smile. Ghost took off for the mountain, with Lucinda's laughing meows echoing in the background. That was ten years ago.

Tonight, as he approached Dolion's house, he silently promised that nobody else he cared for would be hurt by these wicked creatures.

He saw his destination, but before climbing the steps to the front porch, he heard Lucinda call his name from the tree in the front yard.

"Hi, Ghost. Or is it Joel Grey now? I can't seem to remember," she purred sarcastically at him.

"Where is Belle?" Joel demanded, not wanting to engage in small talk.

"She's alive," Lucinda replied, leaping down from the tree. "Whether she stays that way is entirely up to you."

"If you harm her, I will kill you," Joel meowed softly and ominously, meaning every word of it.

Ignoring the threat as would a lion when challenged by a mouse, Lucinda continued, "Tomorrow, we will meet at Obadiah's old cabin, and you will show me exactly where the still is. Then you and your merry little band will go back to wherever it is you came from. This isn't your town anymore."

Joel simply stared at her, saying nothing. Then he glanced back at Dolion's house.

"By the way, your little Protector isn't here," she told him, following his gaze. "She's somewhere where you can't rescue her. So just show me the still and leave town."

"I don't trust you."

"You don't have a choice," she purred arrogantly.

"How about I introduce you to Mittens, our Protector?" Joel said softly. "She'd wipe the floor with you, and you know it."

"If I see anyone but you tomorrow, your precious Belle will never make it home alive. Nobody but me knows where she is, that I promise you." Lucinda knew she was out on a limb with this statement. But she was counting on Jarred not letting the stupid little black cat loose until she was done hustling Joel.

Seeing that her threat had sunk in, she concluded by saying, "I will see you tomorrow in the morning. Right after first cat breakfast. Don't be late."

With that, she jumped out of the tree and brushed by Joel on her way inside the house, leaving him in turmoil.

At that exact moment, the subject of Lucinda's and Joel's conversation was crawling out of the duct in Jared's house. Careful not to drop the register and moving slowly to not make any noise, Belle turned and gently lowered the grate back into place. Then, straightening, she stretched the kinks out and examined her fur, shaking her head. It would be hours of grooming to get clean, but there was no time for that now.

Instead, she sat silently, listening to the house. The only noise was Jarred's loud snoring in the other room and the refrigerator running in the kitchen. After a minute, she was satisfied that Jarred was the only Person in the house and that she was the only one still awake. Cautiously she began to explore.

Jarred had spent a considerable amount of time typing on his computer while Belle waited in the duct. Since she couldn't see the screen, she had no idea what he was working on, but if there was a chance it could help their case, she needed to find out.

Silently, she jumped onto the desk and began her search. There were no papers to be seen, no books or journals, just a laptop that was turned off. Sitting by the computer was a set of house and car keys. Very carefully, Belle tapped one of the keys with her paw. At home in Torrington, she was able to make the screen turn on when she did that. But, unfortunately, this time, nothing happened.

Passing her gaze over the desk once more, she paused a moment and examined the keyring. It had the usual keys you would expect, but it also had a blue thumb drive attached to it. Looking at the computer, the same kind of blue thumb drive was sticking out of the side of the laptop.

Curious, she thought. She knew that her People used these little devices to carry information back and forth to work.

I wonder what Jarred has on his thumb drive? Then, making her decision, she went around the side of the laptop.

Bending over, she got a good grip on the thumb drive with her teeth and pulled gently, only to have the whole computer move. Then, bracing the laptop with her paw and tugging again, the thumb drive popped right out. *I will get this to Anne, and we can see if it is helpful,* Belle thought. *But first, I need to get out of this house.*

She jumped off the desk and began sneaking through the house, careful to not make a sound. The first room she came to was Jared's. She'd heard nighttime sounds coming from his room and had hoped he'd left his window open. Silently she crept past the bed to the open window, only to see it was covered by a screen. Then, pausing to make sure Jared was still asleep, she left the bedroom to continue her exploration.

The kitchen had a door and window, but both were locked up tight. While in the kitchen, Belle heard water dripping from the sink faucet. Leaping carefully onto the counter, being careful to avoid the towers of dirty, crusted dishes, Belle bent over the sink and licked the dripping water until her thirst was satisfied.

Last, she padded into the main room of the house. There was a large front window with a door on the right. But, again, the same vexing problem confronted her; the door was locked, and the windows appeared tightly shut.

Belle began to plan; *I will have to wait and run out the door as soon as he opens it in the morning.* There was a couch, a coffee table, and an armchair with a dust ruffle. The couch was too far away from the door, but the armchair looked just about right. *If I hide behind it, I will be hidden but still able to see the front door,* she thought.

Getting behind the chair, Belle settled in and closed her eyes. She hoped her friends weren't too worried about her, not wanting to cause them grief. She especially worried about Giblet; he was a fretful fusspot about her duties as a Protector.

Oh well, tomorrow is going to be a busy day, she thought before drifting off.

Cat Time:
Ten Years Earlier, Torrington, CT

Today was the day that Joel and his owner were supposed to leave and return home. Last night, like every night before, he slept curled up next to MacKayla, and for the most part, he slept peacefully. That Joel had grown so close to MacKayla had not escaped the notice of his owner or the young couple hosting them.

They all gathered in the entry hall; the People exchanged pleasantries while Joel and MacKayla sat together on the steps watching. The cat carrier was on the floor with its door open. Joel knew he would soon be put in it, and they would leave.

The woman walked over and picked Joel up, but instead of putting him into the carrier, She gave him a long hug and, to Joel's astonishment, put him back down next to MacKayla.

"Be a good cat, Joel. I will miss you," she told him, picking up the empty carrier and walking out the front door.

Joel didn't understand what was happening until the Man and Woman Person hosting them looked down and said, "You're going to stay here now, Joel. We think MacKayla would enjoy having a friend." They both smiled at him and then went back into the kitchen.

Joel looked at MacKayla and meowed, "Did you know about any of this?"

MacKayla meowed back, "I heard them talking the other day, and I knew this was a possibility, but I wasn't sure." Then, beaming, she said, "Welcome to your forever home, Joel."

Joel felt overwhelming gratitude toward MacKayla and the young couple for adopting him. But he felt special appreciation for the woman who had saved him. *I'm glad there are more good People in the world than bad People,* the Russian Blue thought to himself.

Jumping off the steps, Joel ran to the front window. He saw the kind woman who rescued him pulling out of the driveway. She looked up and smiled, and Joel raised his paw and patted the glass. Thanking her from the bottom of his heart for all she did for him.

CHAPTER XVI

Out of the Frying Pan...

Driving slowly up the road in the same direction,
the black cat disappeared; he swung his head
left and right, scanning the shoulder, another killing
on his mind...

Cat Time:
Eighteen Minutes After
the First Cat Breakfast

All the cats, as well as Iko, paced around nervously after breakfast. They were waiting for their People to leave for work. Giblet had wanted to go as soon as they were all awake, only to have Mittens restrain him.

"We can't all leave before the People are out of the house. It would invite too many questions," she cautioned him.

"Well, they better get going soon, or I am going to leave anyway," Giblet meowed.

"They will be out of the house by seven-thirty," Joel confirmed to the group. "They always are."

The People finished their coffee and put the dishes in the sink. Giblet positioned himself in the front window as they headed to the front door. He watched the Man-Person and Woman-Person walk down the street and disappear around a corner. Wasting no time, he headed for the basement and their way out of the house, only to have Mittens slow him down once again. She wanted to give final orders before everyone split up.

"Iko, you stay here and wait with Anne." Iko hung her head low at being excluded, but it was no use arguing with Mittens. Then turning to Joel, Mittens said, "Giblet and I will walk with you to Porter's house, and we will head out from there."

Last night before the meeting broke up, Mittens instructed Porter not to let Joel out of his sight when they were together. "Joel is very fond of Belle. I don't want him running off to do something rash on his own."

The old Highland Collie assured Mittens, "Ah will keep my yaks o' em."

"Yaks?" Mittens asked with a raised eyebrow.

"Eyes! Yee furry little sassenach," Porter replied in a voice that bemoaned the tragedy for anyone who had the misfortune not to be born in the Highlands.

The three cats went down to the basement and out the pet window into the backyard, ready to meet the day's challenges. Soon they were at the front walk leading up to Porter's House. The Highland Collie was not on the porch. "He's probably inside," Joel observed. "I'll go up and meow at the door," he said as he headed up the walk.

"Be careful, Joel," Mittens called after him, watching him approach the front door.

"Come on, Mittens," Giblet said impatiently, already turning to leave.

Mittens wanted to watch and make sure Porter came out, but Giblet wasn't slowing down; he was on his way to the police station, and nothing was going to stop him. Turning one more time back to check Joel, she saw him climbing the steps to the house. *He'll be fine,* she said, trying to reassure herself, and ran to catch up to Giblet.

Just before he reached the door, Joel glanced back to see that Mittens had left. Just like he'd planned, she had gone. Then, without slowing down, he immediately made a ninety-degree turn and ran to the end of the porch. There was only one appointment Joel had any intention of keeping today as he dashed off for Oba's cabin.

Belle was having her own challenges starting her day. Not long after the sun rose, she was awake and ready to make a break for it as soon as Jarred opened the front door. The only problem was that Jarred kept sleeping. She sat behind the chair and listened to him snore, and snore...and snore.

When is this guy going to get up?

Belle could only guess when Jarred finally awoke and began to get ready, but she knew it was late. Thirty or forty cat minutes later, he wandered into the front room wearing a stained uniform and sipping a cup of coffee.

As he reached for the front doorknob, Belle held the thumb drive in her mouth and began her butt-wiggle, getting ready to bolt. As the door opened and she finally saw a clear path to freedom. Careening out from behind the chair, the little cat wove around Jarred's legs and dashed into the yard. Behind her, she heard Jarred fall to the ground and exclaim, "What the hell?" obviously startled at having a cat run under his feet and out of his house.

Belle did not stop, not knowing if Lucinda was around or if Jarred would pursue; her entire focus was to put some distance between her and her captor. She had to get back to town and her clowder as soon as possible and warn them about Lucinda.

Running down the side of the road without a course or idea where she was, Belle's only hope was that she might be heading in the right direction. Not until Jarred's house was well out of sight did she slow down.

Coming to a stop and breathing hard, she looked around to get her bearings. She appeared to be on the only road around; looking up at the Sun, she guessed it ran east and west. *I need to see more of the area,* Belle thought. Picking out a reasonably tall tree, she began to climb, her sharp claws digging into the bark and her legs propelling her upward.

Reaching the top where the branches thinned out, Belle began scanning the horizon for recognizable landmarks. *I know there is a radio tower in Busby that belongs to that country music station. Where is it?* Looking across the horizon, she spotted it, poking just above the trees in the distance.

"The sun is behind me, and that is east, and the tower is west of me... my house should be right about there," she said to a bird chirping at her from the neighboring branch.

The bird, for its part, was unimpressed with Belle's triangulation and instead wanted to know when this noisy cat was going to leave its tree. "Chirp, chirp, chirp!"

"Okay, I'm going," Belle meowed as she started back down. Once she reached the ground, she paused to decide the best route. *I could follow the road or go through the woods,* she thought. The road would be easier but add time to the journey, and Jarred might spot her. The straight line through the woods would be faster, but it presented its own trials, not least of which was probably getting lost. In the end, the quicker route won out. After all, time was of the essence.

While Belle was reconnoitering her path home, Jarred was frantically searching his house for the blue thumb drive that was supposed to be in his laptop's USB port.

Thirty minutes before, he was sitting on the front porch after being tripped, watching the black cat from the cellar disappear up the road. "How in the hell did that stupid cat get in here?" he exclaimed to no one. Then, calling out after the retreating animal, he shouted, "I hope you get run over and squashed flat or eaten by a fox." *That is why I don't like cats,* the police chief thought. *Always sneaking around, always into other people's business. And what on earth was that blue thing in that cat's mouth?*

After getting up and dusting himself off, he reached for his keys that had fallen on the concrete slab outside his front door. That's when he froze. That blue thing in the cat's mouth looked just like the thumb drive he kept on his keyring. *Nah, that couldn't have been the laptop thumb drive. Why in the world would a cat take that? It isn't food; it isn't a toy, so why would a cat take it?*

Jarred walked back into his little office and stared in horror at the laptop's empty USB port. He remembered entering this week's payoffs into the computer and saving the file to both thumb drives. Usually, when he was done entering his notes, he would hide the backup drive under the kitchen sink. However, last night he was tired and decided to go to bed, leaving the thumb drive in the computer.

He looked all over the room and then the house, trying to find the drive. He pulled the couch apart, checked under the armchair, and even searched the kitchen and bathroom, finding nothing. By the end of the search, his heart was pounding in his chest, and the situation was becoming increasingly desperate.

"That thumb drive has EVERYTHING on it," he screamed to an empty house. "Why in the hell did that cat steal it? It's only a stupid animal; how would it know that thumb drive was important?" One more search of the house only reinforced what he already knew, the thumb drive was gone, and the cat took it.

Really sweating now, Jarred went out to his police car and sat for a few minutes, thinking. Then, reaching for the police radio, he needed to call in. However, his hands were shaking so bad that he needed both of them to hold the microphone. "Dispatch, this is Chief Jarred. I've got some errands to run and won't be in for a while."

"Confirmed, Chief," came the reply.

Pulling out the same gun he used to kill Obadiah, Jarred chambered a forty-five-caliber round and cocked back the hammer of the Colt 1911. Then, setting the pistol carefully on the passenger seat beside him, he began driving slowly up the road in the same direction the black cat disappeared; all the while, his head swung left and right, scanning the shoulder, another killing on his mind.

Mittens and Giblet arrived at the Police Station; however, there was no sign of Jarred or his car.

"Where is he?" Giblet meowed with worry.

"I have no idea," Mittens answered. "Let's give it a few minutes."

Both cats picked a spot where they could see most of the front of the Station and some of the back parking lot. Mittens knew that stakeouts were often tedious; in the course of her career as a Protector, she had done many of them. So she made herself comfortable and let her gaze travel back and forth, looking for anything out of the ordinary that could be a clue. Giblet, on the other hand, couldn't settle down. He was pacing back and forth, getting more agitated with each passing moment.

Not taking her eyes off the police station, Mittens said, "I know it's hard, but you have to calm down; save your strength. You will need it before this day is done."

Ignoring the advice, the tomcat said, "I'm going down there to that open window. I'm going to listen for anything that might help."

Mittens knew he was going to do it whether she agreed or not, and knowing that Giblet would be less conspicuous than a large Maine Coon, she nodded in agreement.

Giblet ran toward the dumpster at the back of the station. He hopped on the lid and then onto the open window's sill. He sat and listened for almost five minutes before jumping down and returning to Mittens' side.

"He called in that he was going to be late," Giblet reported. "What do you suppose that means?"

"I don't know," she admitted. "Did they say anything else?"

"From how they talked, Jarred isn't on time most days." Then, as an afterthought, Giblet added, "And they really don't like him."

Nodding, Mittens suggested, "One of us should stay here, and the other should go check out Dolion's funeral home and bar; see if Jarred is there."

"I will stay," Giblet said immediately. "When Jarred shows up, I will check out the car."

"Okay," Mittens agreed. Then, looking up at the sun and gauging the time, she said, "I want us to meet back at the house at noon and report. We may have to change our plans to find our wayward Protector."

"Okay," he promised.

Mittens headed off for Dolion's businesses as Giblet settled in, a worried look lining his face.

As Mittens approached the funeral home, Belle was emerging from the woods. Looking around, she saw she was up the street from her house.

Yes! Not a bad bit of navigation, she thought to herself and began running down the street to the house. She crawled through the pet window and ran upstairs to the kitchen to see who she could find.

Iko and Anne were in the kitchen when the bedraggled black cat came bounding in. The dog and human leaped to their feet and began shouting questions at her.

"Belle! Where have you been?"

"We've been worried sick."

"How did you escape?"

"Is Giblet with you?"

"You're a mess!"

Glancing at her fur, Belle saw she was covered in brambles, dirt, and some lingering grime from that old duct. *I do look like a feral cat coming off a three-day bender at that,* she agreed. She tried to respond, but her meow came out as a croak instead.

She immediately jumped up and dropped the thumb drive on the table. Then she managed one word to Anne, "Water?" Quickly, Anne filled a bowl from the kitchen sink and set it before her, along with a small bowl of kibble. The only sound for the next few minutes was the lapping of water by the parched black cat and the crunch as she ate some of the kibble.

While Belle was drinking and eating, Anne picked up and scrutinized the thumb drive. "What's this?" she asked.

After Belle had had her fill for the moment, she replied, "That is from Jarred's computer. I don't have any idea what's on it, but he was typing on the computer most of last night."

"Everyone has been really worried," Iko woofed at her. "How did you get away?"

"Believe it or not, I had to crawl through another duct," Belle meowed, grinning at her own cleverness. "Where is everybody?"

"They are all out looking for you," Anne responded. "Giblet and Mittens are at the Police Station looking for Jarred. Joel is out with Porter; they are searching for you also."

"Joel went out alone?" Belle asked, with worry in her voice.

"No, he left with Mittens and Giblet. They were supposed to meet up with Porter." Iko woofed.

Anne didn't understand what Iko was saying but saw Belle get an apprehensive look on her face. "What is it?" she asked.

"Dolion's cat, Lucinda, was behind my catnapping. Jarred threw me in his cellar, and Lucinda bragged that she was going to make Joel show her where Oba's old still was hidden." Then, thinking fast, she added, "Are you sure Joel is with Porter right now?"

Human and dog both shook their heads. "Mittens and Giblet left with Joel so they could walk with him," Iko informed her. "We don't know what happened after that."

Getting to her paws, Belle announced, "I'm going to Porter's."

"I coming with you," Iko announced.

"Thanks, Iko, but you need to stay here and let the others know what is going on."

"The human lady can do that," Iko protested. "Besides, I want to help, and you might need backup."

Anne was only catching one side of the conversation. But instinctively knew that Iko wanted to go with Belle. "It's okay, Belle. I will cover for all of you. Take Iko and be careful."

Since Iko couldn't go through the pet window downstairs, Anne walked them over and opened the front door; she watched as the cat and the dog disappeared up the street. Then, returning to the kitchen, she booted up her computer and plugged in the thumb drive. Soon she was scrolling through the files she found, her eyes growing wider with every page she skimmed.

"Son of a gun," Anne muttered to herself after reading for over two hours. Then she reached for her cell phone.

CHAPTER XVII

Into The Fire...

"NOOOO…" came a cry from the mine entrance.
Lucinda turned her head as a black blur came at her.

Cat Time:
High Noon

Belle and Iko bounded up to Porter's house. Porter was sitting on his front porch and got to his paws when he saw them.

"Ye are back, ah see," the Highlander said to Belle. " But, where's Ghost?" he questioned, looking behind them for his old friend.

"He hasn't shown up?" Belle asked hurriedly.

"Nae, aye been waitin' since morn. Where ye been?"

"Listen, Porter," Belle began. "Lucinda captured me yesterday, and she had Jarred hold me all night. I just escaped this morning. She said she was going to make Joel take her to Obadiah's still."

"I think as soon as Joel shows her the still, she is going to kill him," Belle finished up.

Iko listened to both sides and began the same pacing Giblet had done, not wanting to wait but wanting to do something. Finally, she barked, "Come on, we got to find Joel!"

"Noo jist haud on," Porter replied. "Whit do ye have in mind?"

Belle took a deep breath and closed her eyes for a moment. Mittens' lessons came rushing back to her; a *leader can be wrong, just never unsure.* The young Protector opened her eyes and immediately came up with a plan.

"Porter, you're going to take me to Oba's mine and still. We need to make sure Joel is safe. Iko, I want you to stay here in case Giblet or Mittens show up so you can tell them where we have gone.

"You're gonna need me," the Australian Cattle dog implored. "I should come."

"I agree that we could use you," Belle meowed. "You're a strong, resourceful dog. But somebody needs to stay here and tell the others, and there is nobody I would trust more than you. Besides, I need Porter to take me to the mine; we don't know where it is."

Being the only dog in a house full of cats who were constantly involved with adventure made Iko feel a little left out; whenever they ran off, She had to remain behind. She longed to be part of the group.

Understanding the responsibility that Belle was placing on her, Iko nodded and said, "I will wait here and tell whoever shows up what is happening. Belle's confidence in her made her feel like a full member of the team for what really was the first time in her life.

I will follow you to the mine when Giblet or Mittens shows up." Then, seeing the question in Belle's eyes, Iko replied, "I will follow your scent."

Nodding her head at her friend, Belle turned to Porter and asked, "Are you ready?"

"Aye, let's git this show on."

Together they headed up the mountain to save Joel.

For his part, Joel had been waiting at Oba's old cabin since he ditched meeting Porter. Sitting there, staring at the ruin and feeling very old and melancholy, he wished he could have stayed away from here more than anything. Then, after a while, he heard soft paw falls coming up behind him. He didn't need to turn his head because a voice purred, "Glad you made it Ghost." The voice was layered with sarcasm and malice.

Lucinda sat down beside him and stared at what was left of the cabin. "It would have been better if you and Oba had just taken Dolion's offer. What a waste," she said, shaking her head.

Not responding, Joel got up and began walking up the mountain. "Let's go," he said.

The last time I went this way, Oba was with me, Joel thought to himself. This time he got to listen to the taunts from Lucinda as they walked.

"You used to be something, Ghost. You were a king in this town. We could have ruled together. And now look at you, an old tired house cat. My, how the mighty have fallen."

Joel kept his peace and continued to the mine. He knew that his silence would ruffle her more than any retort he could come up with. One thing Lucinda hated was being ignored.

"I give you full marks for hiding the still," she said to the back of Joel's head. "I must have looked over this mountain a hundred times in the last ten years, but I never found it."

Soon they came to the little cleft in the mountainside with a large boulder. Walking around the boulder, for the first time in over ten years, Joel went into Obadiah's and his mine. Of course, there was nobody to light the hurricane lamps anymore, so the soft light that made the mine a cozy place was absent, but Joel's cat eyes had no problem seeing everything in the main chamber.

There it was: the old Still. It was cold and covered in dust and spider webs, but the sign on its side, put on by Oba with care and love, was plainly visible. For her part, Lucinda came in and saw the inscription Joel was staring at. Callously, she chuckled and began walking around, taking stock of what was in the mine.

"Where's the recipe for the shine, Ghost?" she called out as she continued exploring the various chambers.

"You stupid cat," Joel erupted, getting angry and finally breaking his silence and reverie. "It was in Obadiah's head. That was lost when your idiot owner and Jarred shot him! Now, tell me where Belle is so I never…"

Joel never completed the thought because something that felt like a club hit him on the side of the head, staggering him. For a moment, he wondered what it was. Did a piece of the mine ceiling fall? However, the uncertainty of what happened was put to rest when he turned his head and saw Lucinda raise her paw again and clout him across the nose with her claws. He heard, what was to him a thunderous crack, and blood immediately began flowing.

As a young cat, Joel had gotten into more than a few scrapes and wasn't a half-bad fighter. Trying to shake off the dizziness, he tried to counter-attack when suddenly, something that felt like a furry bowling ball smashed into him, knocking the wind out of him and crashing him into the metal side of the still. Joel was now completely stunned and unable to catch his breath. Lucinda stood over him and began swiping him with her claws, opening deep gashes. As Joel started to pass out, he heard Lucinda's cruel laugh.

"Hurry, Porter, we have to get there," Belle pleaded with the Highlander. For his part, Porter was moving as fast as he could; however, he wasn't all that young anymore and had not made this trek since Oba died.

"Keep the heid!" He said, trying to catch his breath. "I'm fair puckled."

Belle guessed that Porter meant that he was out of breath. Seeing him panting so hard made her feel bad about pushing him, but her cat sense was telling her that Joel was in danger.

"How much farther?" she asked. "If you tell me, I can go on ahead, and you can catch up."

After another hundred yards, Porter had to sit. Then, panting even hard, he apologized and said, "Sorry, I'm loused, pure done in."

"Where is the mine from here?" she asked, not wanting to risk Porter any further.

The Highland Collie pointed with his nose and said, "Straight up that way, a couple of hundred yards. Ye will see a wee cleft in the groond. Ta mine is behind a boulder."

"Okay, you stay here and rest," Belle said. "Tell any of the others who show up where I am."

"Bide yerself wee one. That Lucinda's heart is black as the Earl of Hell's waistcoat."

"I will. Wish me luck," and with that, Belle began running up the mountain to rescue Joel.

Joel was a mess, and he knew it. He had numerous deep scratches, a broken nose, and he was sure several of his ribs were cracked. Lucinda had paused in her attack and was looking at her handy work. Joel opened his eyes and looked at her without fear.

"You are going to be an example, Ghost," she said triumphantly. "I made you an offer, and nobody turns me down!" she cackled, sounding quite mad. Joel, for his part, just looked at her with pity.

"I will make this quick," Lucinda said as she moved into position to snap his neck.

"NOOOO..." came a cry from the mine entrance. Lucinda turned her head as a black blur came at her.

CHAPTER XVIII

No Quarter Asked
or Given...

"You have hurt my friends," Mittens growled.
"You have hurt other animals. This ends today."

Cat Time: The End and the Beginning...

A hammer is not that impressive. It is an ancient tool; on average, modern hammers weigh a mere twenty ounces, a modest sum for the job it does. The average hammer's head is less than one and a half inches in diameter, and the handle averages fourteen to sixteen inches. When the hammer is swung, that swing builds to an average speed of twenty-nine meters per second, or about sixty-five miles per hour. All that kinetic energy and force is transferred to a five-sixteenth-inch nail head with the approximate equivalent of a hundred pounds of force. The energy transfer is known as Work Done, and Work Done = Force × Distance. That is why even a modest hammer can drive a nail into hardwood by people with typical strength.

Belle launched herself at the Persian cat from a distance of five feet, focusing all her mass and momentum into a one-paw-size point of contact, just like she was taught. All of her built-up kinetic energy would hit the target with impressive force if done right. Belle's aiming point was Lucinda's head, specifically the orbito-sphenoid bone of the skull, just behind the eye and below the ear; it is one of the thinnest places on a cat's skull.

And, she missed.

At the last moment, the Persian Cat moved just enough so that the blow landed on her shoulder instead of her head. Still, the force of the impact knocked Lucinda head over tail away from Joel. Belle tucked into a roll and ended up between her and Joel, back arched and claws ready.

Picking herself up, Lucinda glared at the smaller Protector and meowed, "I might have known that that idiot Jarred would let you go."

"Clear out of here, Lucinda," Belle hissed. "You are not getting near Joel.

"Belle, leave. Get out of here," Joel said, barely above a whisper from where he was lying behind her. "She's mad; she'll kill you."

Belle let out a loud, angry hiss at Lucinda and held her ground. For her part, Lucinda approached the black cat carefully, not discounting the abilities of any creature fighting for its life.

Belle and Lucinda circled each other, each looking for an opportunity to exploit. Lucinda's attacks were powerful and deadly, but Belle's speed and youth meant they did not land. On the other hand, the blows Belle did land caused minimal damage to such a large foe.

Again they circled, hissing and spitting at each other. The problem was that Belle was tiring. She had already run a great distance that day and had not slept well the night before. *I better come up with an idea soon,* she thought. *I don't know how much longer I can keep this up.*

Belle decided to make a daring move and leaped almost straight up; her goal was to land on the Persian's back and dig in all four sets of claws. If she did it right, her opponent's neck would be open for her to clamp down on with her impressive fangs.

Unfortunately, Lucinda was ready for that move. She dropped and rolled over, kicking out with her back legs. She caught Belle in the air before she could land and sent her crashing to the ground by Joel. To her credit, Belle rolled over and came to her feet, relatively unharmed but completely winded. The Persian saw that Belle was almost at the end of her reserves and began advancing on her slowly.

"This is where it ends for both of you, little Protector," Lucinda said with a smile. Then she stopped because Belle was not looking at her but at something behind her. Then a voice introduced herself from behind, "Hi Lucinda, I'm Mittens."

Turning her head, Lucinda saw what only could be described as the most immense Maine Coon paw she had ever seen coming straight at her head. The blow caught her across the side of her skull, staggering her. Before she could process that, another paw flashed out and clocked the other side of her head. She stumbled back only to be grabbed, held, and rabbit-kicked hard and repeatedly in the stomach, so powerfully that it knocked the wind out of her. Finally, Mittens kicked out and sent the Persian flying into the mine wall, falling and coming to rest on the hard-packed floor.

"You have hurt my friends," Mittens' growled. "You have hurt other animals. This ends today."

The two cats began circling each other, slashing and spitting. However, Lucinda was the only one to suffer any damage. Mittens was able to counter or turn away each of the Persian's attacks and followed each one up with a withering response.

The number of real fights Mittens had ever got into could be counted on one paw. And, even then, she would hold back, not wanting to hurt her opponent very much. Belle watched in amazement as her teacher fought Lucinda; she could tell Mittens was not holding back this time.

Slash, spit, hiss, the fight continued. As it became apparent that Lucinda would not win against Mittens, she became increasingly possessed and deranged. Finally, she ranted at Mittens, "This is *my town*. You are nothing! I've killed Protectors before!" she howled. Crouching low, Lucinda leaped straight at the Maine Coon, her front claws extended.

MACLEARN
DISTILLERY
EST. 1885
OBIDIAH & CHESTER
PROPRIETORS

Mittens halted the advance, but in the process, Lucinda scored a wicked slash across her muzzle. Mittens took the blow, shook it off, and then took the Persian's left eye with a precise slash of her front claws.

At that point, Mittens disengaged and backed away to stand with Belle. Above all, Mittens was, first and last, a Protector. She wouldn't take a life if she could help it. "It's over, Lucinda. Yield," she hissed.

Lucinda rolled over to her paws, blood coursing down her face. Then, laughing insanely, she ran toward the mine entrance only to come to a halt. The opening was blocked by Porter and another dog she had seen briefly; both were growling and baring their canines; a tabby cat was between them, also hissing menacingly, ready for battle.

Lucinda turned on the spot and ran back as fast as she could past Mittens and Belle, disappearing deeper into the mine.

"She's getting away," Belle announced.

"No. she isn't," came Joel's weak voice. He knew exactly what awaited her. A few moments after disappearing into the inky darkness of the mine, all of the animals heard a terrible animal shriek, followed a moment later by a muffled crash from somewhere deep in the earth. Lucinda had fallen into the abandoned shaft at the back of the mine.

"Oba said that shaft goes down well over a hundred people feet," Joel said in a whisper. "She ain't comin' back from that."

"Oh Joel, we need to get you home," Belle said, looking over her friend. "Maybe we can get Anne, and she can get a box and carry you."

"No, little one. I am home," Joel said, his breathing labored. Belle and the rest of the animals gathered around.

"What? I don't understand?" Belle exclaimed. "What do you mean? I promised MacKayla I would protect you."

Over Joel, the luminescent glitter appeared in the air. Suddenly Belle knew what was happening. "NO, Joel! You can't go. You're coming home. I needed to protect you...You will get well, and we will all be a family again."

Mitten and Giblet understood what was happening and smiled so Joel could see them. Iko and Porter also caught Joel's eye. Together, they bowed their heads to the Russian Blue in a dog's most sincere sign of respect. Only Belle wasn't having any of it.

"No, Joel," Belle said again, tears streaming down her whiskers. "Please…please…"

Giblet went up to Belle and stood by her, stroking her fur with his paw. "It's okay, Belle, it's Joel's time."

Joel looked up at the glitter and smiled. Then, whispering to Belle, he said, "It's okay, Belle. It's oka…"

Above their heads, a doorway into the infinite opened, and a voice came through that only a cat or dog could ever hear, "Come on, Ghost, you old rascal. Time's a-wastin'."

Looking up, all the animals saw a man with a beard and kind eyes, smiling down; standing next to him was MacKayla. Mittens and Giblet recognized MacKayla instantly and smiled. Porter's tail wagged furiously at the sight of Obadiah as he sat up, waving his paws.

A moment later, a gray cat was standing at Oba's side. Ghost was young, healthy, and with Oba once again. Then the spectral images turned and walked back into the light. But before they vanished, Joel turned his head and looked directly at Belle. He smiled and nodded his head in a way that let her know this was right, this was what he wanted, and he was happy. Finally, the doorway closed, and the mine was once again dark; the only sound was Belle's soft crying.

CHAPTER XIX

Loose Ends

Where is the thumb drive, you stupid cat?" the chief
practically screamed, pointing the gun at Belle.
"What have you done with it?'

Cat Time:
One cat week later.

Mittens and Belle had stayed with Joel's body while Giblet and
Iko returned home to let Anne know what had happened. Then, a
little while later, she appeared at the mine's entrance with a box and
soft towel.

She listened to Mittens explain about the fight and how Joel had died.
Anne paused a moment to look at the old still and saw the inscription
under ten years of dust. Seeing Ghost's name, she commented, "Joel sure
had a full life."

"He did, indeed," Mittens meowed. Then, respectfully, Anne
scooped Joel up and placed him in the box. As she carried him home,
all the animals divided up, some walking in front and some behind, an
honor guard for a lost friend.

When the family arrived home with the kids later that day, Anne
told them that Joel had gotten out of the yard and was attacked by a wild
animal and had died, which was the truth, more or less. The Children

and the mom all began crying at the news; even Iko howled in response to all the sadness around them.

The Man-Person wanted to give Joel a decent burial, so he called Marie, the house owner, and explained what had happened. He asked her if they could bury Joel in the corner of the backyard.

"We would really like to have a little service for Joel," Russell Macgregor said on the phone. "Joel has been around since before the kids were born."

"I understand completely," Marie replied. "Obadiah never turned an animal away who needed help. He would have been happy to offer up his yard for this. Joel even looked like his old cat, Ghost."

That evening, the Man-Person dug a hole near some beautiful flowers. The Woman-Person put Joel in a clean cardboard box with one of his toys, and each of the Children added a token of love.

They all gathered around and laid Joel to rest. The Man-Person and Woman-Person recalled how he had come to live with them and how he had bonded with MacKayla, their first cat.

The cats and Iko watched from the back porch in respectful silence, knowing that Joel/Ghost would have been happy with the simple service. Unfortunately, Porter could not be present. All the animals agreed that his attendance would have raised too many questions.

Porter understood. "Ah will pay ma respects wen ta People gan asleep," he assured the others.

Finally, the hole was filled in, and the family went back inside with most of the animals. Only Belle remained outside and continued to stare at the grave. Then, after a while, she sensed a cat approaching, "I don't want to talk about it, Giblet," she meowed without turning.

"I am not going to talk. I was just going to sit with you for a while if that's okay," he purred at her.

Belle didn't acknowledge Giblet's remark and continued to stare at the grave. Taking her lack of any response as an affirmative, he settled next to her to continue the silent vigil.

It had been a week since Joel/Ghost had passed over the Rainbow Bridge, and the family was still grieving and planning their return trip to Torrington.

The Man-Person finished his local research on various aspects of the production and sale of homemade whiskey. Along the way, he had secured a dozen excellent interviews with locals who provided in-depth background on the history of distilling in Busby; their colorful anecdotes about the ole days of making shine and bootlegging added to his understanding of the culture. Furthermore, the free samples of their shine made the interviews very enjoyable.

Throughout his time researching the book and interviewing people, Professor Macgregor had half expected to receive a knock on the door and a visit from the town's police chief, especially after the warning he had gotten when they first arrived. However, the Busby police chief, who had made such a fuss about bothering people with questions, had never said another word about the matter. Instead, quite the opposite happened.

Professor Macgregor had tried several times to engage the police chief for an interview on the lawman's view on the private distillation of whiskey and sales by Busby residents, only to have each message ignored. He had even gone so far as to stop by the police department several times to see if he could interview the chief. Each time he was told that Chief Hebeto wasn't in and wasn't expected.

The town rumor mill, always on the lookout for good gossip, was chattering away about the condition of Chief Hebeto. Townspeople who encountered the chief over the past week commented that it looked like the chief hadn't shaved or bathed in some time. Besides the general deterioration of his appearance, people mentioned that the chief was driving around town at all times of the day and night, looking for something. Finally, when several concerned citizens walked up to his patrol car to ask the chief if anything was the matter, a clearly agitated

Chief Hebeto proceeded to question them at length about the whereabouts of a smallish black cat, who was very sneaky, perhaps carrying a blue thumb drive in its mouth.

The citizens assured him that they hadn't seen any black cats with thumb drives but would call immediately if they did. Then, one after another, they backed slowly away from the patrol car with forced smiles on their faces. Soon thereafter, the entire episode was posted on social media.

The general consensus was that the pressure of the job was getting to the chief, but in a town of fewer than a few thousand residents and only two stoplights, the next thought naturally was what pressure? Moreover, in a community not wanting for eccentric characters, the chief was quickly becoming the clear standout and was raising the bar for the next contender.

The cats mostly stayed out of the way as the family began packing and putting things right in their temporary house. The Man Person had decided he would put the stair post cap back on himself, so Marie wouldn't have to do it or pay someone else to do it.

"Are you sure you can handle it?" the Mom Person quipped.

"Ho-ho and har-har," came the response.

The Man-Person found some tools in the basement and began trying to re-seat the newel post cap. Unfortunately, he couldn't get the cap to sit straight. Mittens and Giblet watched from the steps as the repair progressed.

"He doesn't see the nail sticking out, does he?" Mittens meowed.

"Nope," Giblet agreed.

The Man-Person checked the newel cap, and it looked fine. Then he studied the top of the post, where he saw a tiny nail that was sticking up just a little, effectively stopping his repair.

"There, he's got it now," Mittens observed, and Giblet nodded.

A pair of pliers made quick work of the nail, and once again, he test-fitted the cap, a perfect fit. The Man Person took the cap off one more time and brushed a little dust off, preparing to finish the repair. But, before he sealed it up, he cast a glance down into the cavity of the newel post and stopped cold. What looked like a bundle of rolled-up papers was at the bottom of the post.

Curiosity is not an affliction just for cats. Mittens and Giblet watched as the Man Person got a wire coat hanger, straightened it out, and fished the papers out of the post. A quick glance at the type of paper and coverings assured him that these were very old. Carefully, he carried them to the kitchen table for a closer look, both cats following.

"What have you got there?" his wife asked, sitting with Anne at the kitchen table having a cup of tea.

"No idea. It was in the newell post," he responded.

Setting it carefully on the kitchen table, he unwrapped the leather string around the bundle and delicately unrolled the papers. Scanning the documents quickly, a smile spread across his face. Then, he said to his wife, "Call Marie. Tell her to come over quick. We found something she might be interested in."

It was Friday, their last full day in Busby, and the Macgregors had decided to take a day trip to one of the countless beautiful state parks that West Virginia had to offer. Even though the family had been there for almost three months, they had not gotten to do much except work. Anne was invited to go but decided to stay home, look after the animals, and take it easy.

It was a warm, late summer afternoon, and Anne made herself comfortable on the rocking chair on the porch. As far as vacations go, this one wasn't as restful as she had hoped. However, as she sipped her iced tea and read her book, today was turning out okay.

Later on, the only other thing on Anne's agenda was a walk, so she brought the walking stick out with her and propped it against the rail. The animals were lounging around relaxing; even Porter had come down from his house to enjoy the afternoon and say goodbye to his new friends.

The conversation gradually turned to shared stories about Ghost/Joel, with everyone sharing a personal anecdote. Only Belle held herself apart, not wanting to participate.

"...And then the People-Kittens dressed Joel up as an elf," Mittens continued, to the great amusement of all. "Of course, he took it all in stride. I think he enjoyed having little People-Kittens around."

"He was a good cat," Iko woofed, and the cats and Porter all nodded their heads in agreement.

Belle continued to be despondent about Joel's passing. Mittens glanced at her student sitting alone, wanting her to come over and engage. However, she decided not to press it. If this melancholy persisted after they returned to Torrington, she would have a talk with her student. Until then, she decided to leave her be.

A police car was coming up the street slowly. Belle glanced at it and thought the officer was on regular patrol. However, as soon as it got close, she recognized it immediately as Jarred's car. She was about to meow a warning to her friends when the car locked its wheels and came to a screeching halt in front of their house. A clearly agitated and disheveled Chief Hebeto jumped from the vehicle with his gun in hand and walked toward the porch while pointing the pistol at Belle.

All the animals stopped what they were doing and turned in the direction of the sound. Anne also looked up from her book at the noise, not yet understanding the depth of what was unfolding. As soon as she saw the gun, she hit a few buttons on her cellphone and sat it on the table in front of her.

"Where is the thumb drive, you stupid cat?" the chief practically screamed, pointing the gun at Belle. "What have you done with it?'

Belle looked at the gun and the irrational person holding it and slowly got to her paws. With the utmost caution, she began moving slowly to her right. Her goal was to ensure her friends were well out of the line of fire.

Iko and Porter gave low growls, but Mittens caught their eye and shook her head. "Stay calm," she softly meowed. Then, she patted Giblet on his shoulder and slowly went to the end of the porch, where she could get to the ground without Jarred seeing her. For his part, Giblet stood by the rail and readied himself.

"Officer, I'm Anne Gaumont, retired Senior Detective of the Torrington Police Department," she said, getting slowly to her feet and holding her hands out so he could see she was unarmed. "Please holster that weapon and tell me how I can help you?"

"I'm a chief, not just an officer," he said. "That cat," —he pointed with the gun's muzzle— "stole my thumb drive. I want it back!"

"Chief, that is my cat, and she hasn't been away from the house since we arrived in Busby," Anne said soothingly, in her best hostage negotiating voice. "I think you might be mistaken."

"I'M NOT WRONG!" he screamed. "Everyone is always telling me I am wrong—. You—. Dolion, everybody."

Okay, okay, you are not wrong," she said soothingly. "Can you describe the thumb drive? I will help you look for it."

"It's blue, and that cat took it," he said as he walked to the porch steps, his gun shaking a bit as he pointed at Belle, four feet away. Belle sat stock still, her eyes never leaving Jarred or the hand holding the gun. *If I see him taking up slack on that trigger, I will have to move fast,* she thought.

Meanwhile, Mittens knew she needed to flank Jarred in order to provide support to her friends. So as soon as she got to the end of the porch, she leaped down and began running up the street. When she got to the third house, she quickly crossed the road and began her return. Soon, the Maine Coon was precisely where she wanted to be, directly across from her home and behind Jarred. Slowly and silently, she began her approach, staying in his blindside.

"Chief, I haven't seen any thumb drive, blue or otherwise," Anne said soothingly. "Please, I am unarmed; holster your weapon."

Jarred looked confused. He was sure this was the right cat but couldn't focus his thoughts. For her part, Anne saw the rings under his eyes, the dilated pupils, and the sweaty face; she worried about what the man might be on and if he could be reasoned with. Moreover, the fact that the chief seemed to be swaying back and forth didn't instill her with a great deal of confidence to be able to talk sense into him.

Mittens stopped five feet from Jarred's back and nodded at everyone on the porch; she was ready.

"Chief, let's sit down. Would you like a glass of water? We can figure out what we need to do to help you in your investigation." Anne finished her sentence casually placing her hand on her walking stick, and nodded.

Mittens took two big steps and launched herself onto Jarred's back. Digging her claws into his shoulders. Belle immediately rolled to her left as the gun went off, missing her but putting a large hole in the porch floor. Jarred thrashed around, trying to dislodge whatever was on his back, when something very hard crashed down on his wrist, breaking the ulna right where it connects to the wrist; the gun flew off into the grass. The tactical walking stick came spinning around again and connected with the temporal bone on the right side of his skull. Multicolored lights exploded in Jarred's mind and were quickly replaced by oblivion.

Then the whole world showed up.

"As it turns out, we already had an advanced, active investigation into the mayor and police chief when you sent us that thumb drive," Lieutenant Haskin told Anne, glancing back to the state patrol car where Jarred and Dolion both sat handcuffed in the back seat. The mayor sat glaring at the crowd that had gathered and were taking pictures of him and the police chief sitting next to him.

"Those documents sped up the process for warrants. Tell me again where you found it?" he asked, writing down notes.

"Believe it or not, the cat really did bring into the house," Anne replied. "I have no idea where she got it, but once I saw what was on it, I decided to send it to you."

"Do you think someone gave it to the cat in hopes you would get it?" Lt. Haskins speculated.

"As I told you, I have no idea. But why send it to me?" Anne answered. "I never heard of Busby until this Summer, and I never met Chief Hebeto until he threatened our cat. I just think the cat found it on a sidewalk somewhere and picked it up for some unknown reason."

"Jarred keeps saying the cat stole it."

"Oh, come on," Anne laughed, looking over at Belle. "It's a cat."

Lt. Haskins looked over at the black cat sitting on the porch. For her part, Belle looked back and tilted her head to the side with an expression that said, *What, me?*

"I think someone simply lost the drive, and the West Virginia State Patrol is the beneficiary of the information."

"Well, based on those documents, we executed search warrants on the mayor's house, bar, and funeral home. We arrested him at home as he was packing a suitcase. We were looking for Jarred when you called my cell." Then, changing the subject, he said, "I'm glad nobody got hurt," motioning to the bullet hole in the porch floor.

"Everyone did a good job," Mittens purred at her team.

"I just wish Joel knew we won," Belle said, looking at the sky.

"Aye, he does wee bairn. He does," Porter woofed. Then, turning to leave, he said, "Haste ye back!" and began walking home.

CHAPTER XX

Home Again

"We lost Joel. He has gone over the Rainbow Bridge,"
she said very softly.

Cat Time:
First Patrol, back at home.

All in all, cats, dog, and People were happy to be back home. The MacGregor clan had returned from their day out to find Marie, Anne, and many state patrol personnel at their rental house.

Questions were asked about what happened while they were gone for the day, and answers were given—within reason. In Anne's opinion, there was no need to burden the family with unnecessary details.

Furthermore, before the state patrol left, they let the Children sit in a real Police car, albeit not the one with Dolion and Jarred occupied.

Back in Torrington once again, the family resumed their lives. Anne went home, unpacking commenced, and since nobody had the energy to cook, they called out for pizza. Afterward, the children were bathed and put to bed. Finally, the Man-Person and his wife settled on their couch and had a glass of wine. They talked about their Busby adventure and commented that their lives certainly weren't dull.

After the parents went to bed, Belle got ready for her patrol with Mittens; her melancholy had lessened but was not gone. She saw Mittens sitting on the back porch and walked up, "Are you ready?" she asked.

"Hold on," Mittens responded. "I want to talk to you first."

"What's up?"

"You still think you failed Joel, don't you?" the teacher purred at the student.

"MacKayla told me to help him," Belle replied, staring down at her paws.

"Do you remember seeing Joel going into the next plane, smiling and happy?" she asked.

When Belle nodded, Mittens continued. "Joel was carrying massive guilt with him for years. That kind of burden can be corrosive to the soul. A cat, dog, or Person cannot travel freely into the next existence, carrying all that onus in their heart. But, because of your help and investigation, Joel realized he wasn't to blame for Oba's death, and he was able to travel into the next plane because of you.

"But he still died. He shouldn't have died," Belle said sadly.

"Belle, it was Joel's time, as it will be mine one day and yours sometime far in the future," Mittens purred firmly. "You have to understand that even Protectors can't control everything. You haven't seen death until now. And the death of someone you care about is the hardest to bear.

Being a Protector means you will encounter death more than the average cat. It is probably the most challenging thing we will ever have to deal with. To do our job, we can't let death overwhelm us, while at the same time, we can't get used to it and callous our soul. I need you to understand that."

"I think I do," Belle said, looking Mittens in the face for the first time. "It's difficult."

"Of course it is," Mittens agreed. "However, you are a brave and resourceful Protector, and you will get through it."

"I will never forget Joel," Belle said, looking at the stars.

"I know you won't, and neither will I. But we must cherish the good times and not dwell on the bad. Time has a way of making that easier," the senior Protector admitted, getting up and stretching."

"Right now, I want you to go back inside and rest. Giblet would like to see you, and you have done enough lately. I will do a short patrol and thank some of the animals for their help while we were gone."

Belle looked like she was going to argue but relented instead. "Have a good patrol," she meowed and went back inside.

Mittens moved off the porch and began her rounds. First, she passed Mac's house. The retired police dog wasn't out, but she made a mental note to thank him for watching over the neighborhood while she and Belle were away. *I will thank him tomorrow,* she thought.

Continuing the patrol, she came to her turnaround point when a voice called to her from the bushes, "Mittens, mon amour, you've come back to me."

"Oh, how I have missed you," he continued to tease until he got closer and noticed the tears in her eyes and her lower lip quiver. Then, being far more sensitive than any other animal would have given him credit for, he asked quietly and seriously, "Mittens, what's wrong?"

"We lost Joel. He has gone over the Rainbow Bridge," she said softly, unable to look Gus in the eye.

"I am so sorry," Gus purred, remembering the grey cat with a subtle sense of humor. "I liked him. He was a good cat."

Finally, Mittens could not hold it in any longer; thoroughly exhausted by duty, by being stoic all the time, she looked up at Gus and meowed softly, "Please hold me."

"Come here," he said, holding out a paw. Mittens laid against him and wept for her friend and another loss in her life. "Shh, it's okay. Just let it all out. I'm here," Gus said, holding her and comforting her in the moonlight.

Two months later, a large box arrived at the Macgregor home. The return address showed it came from Busby and was sent by Marie MacLearnan. The cats followed the Man Person as he took the box to the kitchen table to open it. Inside, a note was addressed to the whole family was sitting on a second sealed box.

The Woman-Person took the note and began reading it out loud:

Hello Macgregors!

I miss having you as neighbors; Porter also misses you guys. I thought you would enjoy hearing what happened after you left Busby. The mayor and police chief have been indicted and jailed until their trial. They were charged with capital crimes and were denied bail. Believe it or not, Dolion and Jarred robbed graves. People in Busby are furious. And the Busby Police Department has been disbanded. The state patrol has taken over the police duties for the time being. In addition, we are currently without a mayor, but the town is making it work with a temporary administrator.

On a personal note, it appears Dolion and Jarred killed Uncle Obadiah. The state police forensic unit found his body up on the mountain. They say he was shot from behind, and they matched the bullet to Jarred's gun. I knew he was probably dead, but I didn't think he was murdered. We had a memorial service for him at The Rose. Most of the town showed up. It's nice to have closure. I certainly hope Dolion and Jarred pay for their crimes.

On a happier note, I found Oba's still! Do you remember Nathan from the Rose? He and I followed the instructions on those papers you found and discovered the mine where my family had been making whiskey for the last hundred years. And guess what? There was a lot of whiskey in casks sitting there aging. Some of it is over thirty years old.

I gave the recipe and still to Nathan. He plans on continuing the tradition. As a way of thanking you, enclosed is a case of thirty-year-old Oba's special recipe whiskey. I hope you enjoy it.

Don't be strangers.

Sincerely, Marie & Porter

The Man Person opened the second box to find eight bottles of whiskey, gently enclosed in bubble wrap and packing peanuts.

The Man-Person picked up one bottle and held it up to the light; the clear amber liquid seemed to shine all on its own

"I know what kind of cocktail you will be having later," the woman person joked.

"You said it," he agreed.

"Well, isn't that nice," Giblet purred at Belle and Mittens. "I'm glad for them. Marie and Porter were very nice."

"Are you admitting you had enjoyed this summer?" Belle teased.

"Oh sure, if you ignore the murder, catnapping, and general craziness of the summer, it was a hoot!" Giblet said with layered irony.

Epilogue

The animals displayed various emotions as the family pulled their car into the driveway. Belle was on the windowsill, giving a moment-by-moment report while Iko sat below the window, wagging her tail furiously. Mittens was sitting on the couch, outwardly composed, but inside, she was very excited about the new arrivals. Even Giblet was sacrificing nap time for this occasion. The Macgregors had decided to open their hearts to a new cat that needed a forever home and were finally returning from the Animal Rescue Center with the new family member.

Belle had her nose pressed against the glass as the car rolled to a stop.

"They're here," She meowed to everyone in the front room. "They're opening the doors...Getting out...And...Oh my cat, they have two carriers!"

"Two?" Giblet questioned. "I thought they were only going to adopt one new cat?"

"Never underestimate the emotional pull that a kitten in a cage has on People," Mittens purred.

As soon as they entered the door, Iko ran up, her nose working overtime to try to smell the new cats. However, the family didn't stop in the living room but immediately went upstairs to the spare bedroom.

The Man-Person put down kitten food and water and set the two cardboard carriers on the floor. The family opened each carrier, and the Woman-Person gently lifted the kittens out, putting each one on the floor. Then, she closed the carriers so they would have to mingle. "We will let these two get used to this room and each other before seeing the whole house." Then, she began shooing all those present out of the room.

The three cats and Iko remained in the hallway after the family left, trying to decide what to do.

"I'm going to take a nap before supper," Giblet meowed.

"I want to meet our new family members," Belle said impatiently while Iko wagged her tail in agreement.

"Well then, just push on the door," Mittens suggested. "You know that door never latches."

"Do you think it will be okay?" Belle asked with an inquisitive meow.

"They have to meet us sometime," Giblet purred, his curiosity getting the best of him.

Mittens shrugged, and Belle took that as an affirmative. She gave the bedroom door a gentle push, and it swung open. All three cats and the dog went into the room.

A small black kitten sat in front of one of the box carriers. He sat very straight, with bright eyes and big ears. Before any of the clowder could welcome him, he confidently introduced himself.

"Hello, I am Hamilton A. Cat. I am a domestic short hair, and I am six cat months old. Who are you?" he asked in a high-pitched kitten voice.

Belle looked at Hamilton and was taken aback at such self-assured cattitude in one so young. "Hi, Hamilton. I'm Belle, and that is Mittens," she said, motioning with her paw. Then turning to the other side, she continued, "And this is Giblet. The dog's name is Iko. We're your new forever family."

"Genuinely pleased to meet you," Hamilton squeaked.

"You know, we could be twins," he meowed, looking Belle up one side and down the other. "Except, I'm younger and probably know more than you."

Belle looked at the kitten, unsure she had heard him right, while Giblet giggled in the background.

Then walking up to a totally unfamiliar dog, Hamilton squeaked, "I never met a dog before. You smell funny."

Iko turned her head and looked at the little kitten, unsure how to answer him, but before she could say anything, the Woman-Person's voice came rolling up the stairs from the kitchen; "Dinnertime, everyone."

"Dinner?" Hamilton meowed. "I'm a great chef; I can help with dinner." Then, before anyone could stop him, he ran out of the room and started for the kitchen, letting his nose be his guide.

"Oh, my cat. Should we go after him?" Belle asked Mittens, looking worried.

"No. I don't think he will get into too much trouble," Mittens said while softly laughing. "Why don't you try your luck with the second one," the Maine Coon suggested, motioning to the small tabby cat, sitting in front of her box, chewing on her paw and looking totally bored.

Belle nodded and approached the second kitten to introduce herself. The tiny cat had a round stomach and soft tabby-striped fur. She looked for anything like a little teddy bear.

"Hi, I'm Belle," she meowed. "What's your name?"

The tabby kitten was utterly indifferent to the question and continued to groom herself. Finally, when Belle asked again what her name was, she responded uninterestedly, "They call me Holly-Bear."

"Hi Holly-Bear, I'm Belle, and this is Mittens, Giblet, and Iko. Mittens and I are Protectors and take care of the neighborhood."

"Uh-huh," Holly said after a moment.

"Do you know what a Protector is?" Giblet meowed

"Uh-huh," came the reply.

"Would you like to be a Protector one day," Belle asked, searching desperately for a conversation starter.

Holly-Bear stopped grooming and said, "Meh."

"Meh? What's meh?" Giblet whispered to Mittens.

"I think it is a young cat's way of saying she isn't impressed about Protectors," Mittens suggested.

"Why don't you want to be a Protector?" Belle asked, trying desperately to get more than one-word answers.

"I don't wanna be good; it's no fun."

"Well, what do you want?" Belle asked in an exasperated voice.

"I wanna be bad!" the little kitten meowed.

Belle's mouth fell open as Mittens and Giblet burst into laughter.

The End.

Acknowlegments

My sincerest thanks
to these wonderful people:

Marie Lay–Who reads over one hundred books a year and whose critique is my most valuable resource

Mr. Ross Martinek–Good friend and sounding board

Ms. Gloria Fleming–For her time and culinary help

Sparky–For seeing things that I missed

The Orb–For whom these books are really written

And

Ms. Georgia Dunn–Whose art and creativity continue to inspire me

Illustrations–Natalia Junqueira, Dawn Book Designs
www.dawnbookdesign.com

Type Setting/Layout–Danielle Smith-Boldt, Miss D's Designs
missdsdesigns.wordpress.com

Editor–Ashley Strosnider
ashleystrosnider.com/editing

Hamiltons' Recipe

Hi, I am Hamilton A. Cat.

I am a Chef-Cat and live in St. Louis with my forever family. Dad said I could write something for his new mystery book, so I thought I would give you one of my favorite recipes. But first, let me tell you a little about myself.

I was born in the city of St. Louis. In the beginning, it was just Mom and me. She was a street cat, and we lived in an old box behind a restaurant. Mom took good care of me, and there were always amazing smells in the air from the restaurant.

In the evening, the people who worked in the kitchen kept the back door open for cool air. So mom and I would watch them cook through the screen door as they made dinners for their customers. The Chef would always bring us a little something to eat at the end of the night, and it was always delicious.

One day, Mom didn't come back to our box. I didn't know where she went, and I was a sad kitten for a long time. Life is hard for street cats.

To take my mind off missing her, I studied how the kitchen ran each night. I learned what different positions in a kitchen are and how they prepare meals.

I saw the big man cooking all kinds of things at the grill; things would flame up as he turned the beef, chicken, or whatever he was grilling. It was very exciting.

I saw another person make sauces and soups, and a different person made side dishes. Then, over in the corner was a person who made salads and cold dishes. It wasn't a big kitchen, so everyone helped each other out. Running the whole show was Chef; she would call out orders to the different stations, and they would all reply, "Yes, Chef."

One day, the nice Chef picked me up, and she took me to a no-kill shelter called the **Center for Animal Rescue & Enrichment of St. Louis (CARE STL).** It was becoming winter, and Chef didn't want me to be cold. The People at my new place were very nice, but I was depressed. I couldn't watch Chef and her team cook anymore and saw all those cats and dogs without homes. I was a sad kitten again. Then one day, Dad and Mom showed up and walked up and down the row of cages; they stopped to look at me, and I stuck my paw out to fist-bump Dad. They smiled, and after that, they adopted me!

I heard Dad say that places like CARE STL depended on donations and volunteers, so Dad and Mom gave them a nice people-money gift when they picked me up.

I am a lucky cat. Mom & Dad took me to a nice place and said it was my forever home. There, I have other cats to play with, wonderful bird-watching windows, and best of all, Dad likes to cook! In the beginning, Dad didn't realize I was a chef until that day, he was trying to figure out what to make for dinner. I could see right off that he needed help, so I washed my paws and got to work. At first, he was worried about what I was doing, but the meal turned out great!

So, without further ado, this is my recipe for Artichoke Angel Hair Pasta, ala Hamilton.

Important Note

All you People-Kittens out there, make sure you have your adult-People help you if you try to make this recipe. Besides, it's fun to cook with your family.

This is an easy recipe for a great pasta meal, and the ingredients are not very costly. The artichokes and mushrooms are canned to save time.

3–(7.5 oz) marinated artichokes, quartered (I use Reese Marinated Artichoke Hearts)

2–(4.5 oz) prepared sliced mushrooms (I use Giorgio Sliced Mushrooms).

1–medium yellow onion, diced into about ¼" pieces

3 cloves–fresh garlic, minced

4 tablespoons–salted butter, divided

1½ cups–extra virgin olive oil

1 teaspoon–dried oregano

1 bundle–fresh parsley chopped (dried parsley can be substituted)

1–cup reserved pasta water

Fresh cracked pepper

Kosher salt

Grated parmesan cheese

16 oz–dried angel hair pasta (this will make 6–8 servings or plenty of leftovers).

Fill a 6-quart pot with 4 quarts of water. Add 1 teaspoon of kosher salt to the water and heat the water to a boil. When the water reaches a boil, reduce the heat to low and cover to keep the water hot.

Melt 2 tablespoons of butter over medium-high heat in a large saucepan and add the diced onion and minced garlic. Stir the onion and garlic until the onion becomes translucent (about 6–8 minutes).

When the onion is ready, pour the artichokes and the marinade they came with into the pan. Next, add the olive oil, mushrooms, and oregano to the saucepan. Next, add the remaining two tablespoons of butter, a ½ teaspoon of kosher salt, and ½ teaspoon of cracked pepper. When the pan reaches a low boil, reduce heat and simmer for about 10 minutes.

While the artichokes are simmering, bring the pasta water back to a low boil and add the angel hair. Be sure to slowly add the pasta to the water, so it does not boil over. Cook for about 2–3 minutes until the pasta is al dente.

Drain the pasta into a colander, retaining 1 cup of the pasta water. The reserved pasta water will help the marinade adhere to the noodles.

Mix the pasta, artichokes w/marinade, and a ½ cup of reserved pasta water in a large bowl. Toss until the noodles are covered, and everything is mixed well (note, you can add more pasta water to the dish if you want to thin out the emulsion.

Put the pasta into individual bowls, dust with parmesan cheese, garnish with the chopped parsley and serve.

This is a vegetarian recipe. However, for protein, grilled chicken breast is a wonderful addition.

I hope you and your People family enjoy the dish.

Sincerely,
Hamilton A. Cat

Natalia Junqueira
Dawn Book Designs

The illustrations for all the Giblet & Belle series, including cover designs and the Giblet & Belle website illustrations, are the work of the artist Natalia Junqueira and her company, Dawn Book Designs.

Before we began our collaboration, I interviewed a number of artists. Natalia stood out because she asked thoughtful, pertinent questions about the story, the characters, and my vision. She came up with original ideas on how to stage and draw each scene and was happy to fine-tune them to my wishes. Her front/back covers and spine designs are perfect and give the book the kind of feel I was hoping for.

As an author, you see your characters in your head as you write. So when you find an artist who can bring those mental images to life, it significantly helps the creative process, and I am grateful for that.

I know you will enjoy the finely crafted illustrations in this book and the future shenanigans of Giblet & Belle.

Sincerely,
Robert Lay

To see more of Natalia Junqueira's work, visit Giblet & Belle's website at:
https://gibletbelle.com

Or visit Dawn Book Designs at:
https://www.dawnbookdesign.com

About the Author

The blank page. Only a writer knows the horror of the BLANK PAGE! (Suspenseful music in the background). You don't have to be an internationally followed, world-class Author like me* to experience BLANK PAGE panic; you just have to write.

How are the heroes going to get out of the dungeon? Does Lady Scarlet survive the volcano? Will the Pirates discover the treasure? Will anybody…please, please…anybody read my book? All these thoughts compete for space in the Author's mind while they sit in front of the glowing screen, looking at the blank page.

You are not a writer. You can barely write a grocery list and have the audacity to think you can write a book, People know…they're on to you.

Quick, change the subject. The Editor said you need a new short author biography for this book. Robert Lay lives in St. Louis with his beautiful wife of 30 years, two mostly grown, incredibly accomplished children, four cats, and a crazy dog. He likes writing, thinks he is humorous, and isn't as neurotic as it seems (despite what his wife says), bla, bla bla.

Nuts, I can't stop thinking about the chapter. How does Belle survive the fight…because a miracle occurred? Nobody will believe that. Okay, change of tack. Clear your mind; let's look at our email for a distraction. Hmm, ads and bills. Why don't my friends write to say hi? Oh, My CAT! I haven't been a good friend. Nobody likes me!

I will go over to Breaking Cat News comic strip. Beautiful art, engaging stories, and witty posts from Australia…that will help; besides, I know friendly people there who like me. So why hasn't anyone "Liked" my post about neolithic art, quantum mechanics, and cat ownership? People don't like me here either?

Panic ensues.

It is never a good thing for people to find you sobbing at your computer. Okay, Robert. Just finish this chapter, and you can stop for today. Your Martini awaits. Think…Think…YES! Belle will just…(furious typing ensues). Words flow free and clear like a mountain stream. Who cares about speling mistakes and punctuation errors? These are great words; this is writing!

There, you are finished with the chapter. One Bombay Sapphire Martini coming up. A job well done.

The next day, our hero returns to the computer and brings up his latest contribution to the literary intelligentsia of the world. Reading…seriously, I wrote that? What was I thinking? Reading...Reading…Uh hu, yeah, it's official, this is crap! Backspace and take out this word, no, this whole sentence. Backspace is not enough, highlight entire paragraphs and delete.

Start over.

Blank page…

* "World-class Author?"
"Hush, Marie."

Also by Robert Lay:
Giblet & Belle
The Case Of The Missing Ring

https://gibletbelle.com
gibletbelle@gmail.com

Sneak Peak

One Cat Hour Before Dinner...

Belle crept slowly down the pitch-black hallway of the basement; all of her senses were attuned to any threat. She would stop, control her breathing, and listen every couple of feet. To all appearances, she was alone, but she knew the reality was different. Today's advisory was trained in the ways of a Protector, just like Lucinda from Busby was, but unlike Lucinda, this cat was a male.

Even Mittens didn't know of a male cat having Protector training. "As far as I know, there hasn't ever been one," she admitted. But, of course, that made this mission all the more difficult.

It had been over a year since their return to their house in Torrington, Connecticut, without Joel Grey. Belle still felt the pain of loss when she thought about Joel. However, that emptiness in her was tempered by the knowledge that he was happy and with Obadiah, his first owner.

"Loss is part of life," Mittens's schooled her. "Especially for a Protector." Belle understood that lesson, but it was hard. Joel and Oba were now part of the Infinite. Few cats had ever been contacted by the other side, and fewer still had been approached more than once as Belle had.

What this all meant, Belle was not sure. All that she could say was that it must have happened for a reason. *Patience. The answer will reveal itself in time. Now, get your mind on the job, she scolded herself. Your adversary isn't worrying about metaphysical subjects; he wants to beat you.*

Belle silently shook her head and cleared her mind. She was a full Protector now, not just an acolyte. "Your decisions from this point forward will be your own," Mittens had told her. "That is a heady responsibility for any cat. But you have proven yourself multiple times, and I trust you. Congratulations, Protector Belle."

She scanned the hallway but saw nothing; of course, it didn't help that her opponent was jet black also. Then, up ahead, she saw something sitting against the wall that looked cat-sized. *He wouldn't be this obvious... would he?* She approached the mass slowly, getting lower to the ground and making no sound. When she got within a few feet, she saw that her "opponent" was, in fact, a black towel wrapped around a stuffed toy animal. Silently laughing at herself, Belle stood back up on her paws... That's when the attack came.

A heavy weight landed on her, forcing her back to the floor. Over a year ago, the same thing happened in Busby when Lucinda attacked her. At the time, Belle tried every move she knew to dislodge her opponent, only to come up short. That's why she had been practicing new counter moves for the last year to prevent that from happening again. Of course, when you are the smaller cat in almost every fight, a more extensive arsenal of counter-moves is a must.

Quickly she rotated herself, rolling her opponent off her before he could sink in his claws. She kept the roll going, ending up on her paws once again. *Now,* she thought, *time to put a little distance between us so I can counterattack.* Belle leaped further down the hall, tucked into a forward roll, and came to her feet facing her opponent. Only one problem, the other cat wasn't there. As soon as she sprang away, he had disappeared into one of the side rooms that dotted the hallway. There were doorways on both sides of the hall. Which one had he chosen?

She was familiar with her opponent and knew from observation that he was right-paw dominant. Guessing he had escaped into the room on his right, she followed with the determination that he would not have the upper paw again. Bingo, she heard his breathing as she entered the room.

As soon as she turned towards the sound, he came barrelling at her like a steamroller, determined to use his greater size and weight to the best advantage. Belle was knocked over as the other cat rolled over her and kept going. Getting to her feet quickly, she just had enough time to see him coming at her again. The resulting contact knocked her flat once again.

Being this cat's doormat was getting really old, really fast, Belle thought. Then, an idea came to her, and she called out, "Come on, little kitten, let's see you try that again," she goaded her opponent. She knew from experience that even though he was bigger than her, he was only a little over one People year old (about 8 cat years) and hated to be called a little kitten.

Once again, he came at her like a tank, only this time, Belle was ready. As soon as contact was made, her front paws grabbed him by the shoulders, pulling him down with her as she fell backward. Then, kicking both back legs out against his stomach, she heard the breath rush out of him as she pushed his rear-end high in the air, letting his forward momentum flip him over onto his back. Throughout, Belle held on to her advisory and enjoyed the ride, ending up just where she wanted, up on top, with her jaws clamped to his windpipe.

"Yield Hamilton," she purred good-naturedly at her opponent between clenched teeth.

"I yield," he meowed with annoyance.

"How did I beat you?" Belle asked as she disengaged and then sat, cleaning her fur.

"I'm sure you can't wait to tell me," he huffed, then began cleaning his own fur.

"I made you attack on my terms. You can't let your opponent dictate the fight or fall for their taunts. The key to winning the fight is controlling the encounter." Then she added, "Usually."

"I distracted you with the decoy," Hamilton boasted, looking for any positive in this lesson.

"Yes, the black towel in the hallway was a good idea," she purred. "Full marks."

Then changing the subject, she meowed, "You are getting better."

"I should be winning by now," Hamilton retorted.

"Hamilton, when you realize you don't know everything, you will be able to learn something. I enjoy our training sessions." Belle said and licked his head to show she cared for him.

Part of Hamilton's charm was his pomposity. Since the little black kitten arrived in their home, he had regularly boasted he knew more than any other cat; and just as often was shown that he didn't. When Giblet, a cat of considerable pretentiousness, felt that you were full of yourself, that was a rare achievement.

Still, Hamilton had ingratiated himself to the family and the clowder. "He's a good cat," Mittens had said when Belle suggested giving him some Protector training. "I think that's a good idea."

"Come on, let's go upstairs. The People will be home soon, and you always help with dinner." So together, they climbed the basement steps and padded into the family room. They would be there when their Persons and People-Kittens got home.

Belle had settled on the couch and was reading the newspaper when she heard a cat running down the upstairs hall and then the steps. Hamilton also looked up from his grooming just in time to see Mittens' bolt into the family room.

"Come on, Belle, we have to go. Cassidy is in trouble," Mittens said urgently, heading for the basement and the way out of the house. Cassidy was the oldest People Kitten and should have been at Grandma Gaumont's home next door.

"I didn't hear anything," Belle said, getting to her paws. "How do you know?"

"Because she cried out to me in my mind," the senior Protector exclaimed.

"Oh, my cat," Belle and Hamilton replied simultaneously.

Be sure to come back for Giblet & Belle's next adventure.

Giblet & Belle
The Case Of The Vendetta
Coming Soon